PRAISE FOR

The Popper PENGUIN RESCUE

"Quite **delightful**." —*Kirkus Reviews*

"Bringing a contemporary conscience to its predecessor, the wholesome book champions respect for animals and environmental issues within the structure of a **satisfying family adventure**." —*Publishers Weekly*

"There are plenty of affectionate callbacks to the original Popper tale, but Schrefer's story is an **entertaining adventure** of its own.... It's a joy to have Popper penguins back to play." —*Booklist*

The Popper
PENGUIN
RESCUE

Inspired by the Newbery Honor Book
Mr. Popper's Penguins
by Florence and Richard Atwater

BY ELIOT SCHREFER
ILLUSTRATED BY JIM MADSEN

LITTLE, BROWN AND COMPANY
New York Boston

Little, Brown and Company
Hachette Book Group
1290 Avenue of the Americas, New York, NY 10104
Visit us at LBYR.com

Originally published in hardcover and ebook by Little, Brown and Company in October 2020
First Trade Paperback Edition: September 2021

Little, Brown and Company is a division of Hachette Book Group, Inc.
The Little, Brown name and logo are trademarks of Hachette Book Group, Inc.

The publisher is not responsible for websites (or their content)
that are not owned by the publisher.

The Library of Congress has cataloged the hardcover edition as follows:
Names: Schrefer, Eliot, 1978– author. | Madsen, Jim, 1964– illustrator. | Atwater, Richard. Mr. Popper's penguins.
Title: The Popper penguin rescue / by Eliot Schrefer; illustrated by Jim Madsen.
Description: First edition. | New York: Little, Brown and Company, 2020. | "Inspired by the Newbery Honor Book Mr. Popper's Penguin by Richard and Florence Atwater." | Audience: Ages 8–12. | Summary: Long after Mr. Popper found his famous penguins a proper home, his distant relatives, Nina and Joel, move to a new house with their mother and find mysterious eggs in the basement.
Identifiers: LCCN 2020005068 | ISBN 9780316495424 (hardcover) | ISBN 9780316495417 (ebook) | ISBN 9780316495448 (ebook other)
Subjects: CYAC: Penguins—Fiction. | Single-parent families—Fiction. | Moving, Household—Fiction. | Arctic regions—Fiction. | Humorous stories.
Classification: LCC PZ7.S37845 Pop 2020 | DDC [Fic]—dc23
LC record available at https://lccn.loc.gov/2020005068

ISBNs: 978-0-316-49540-0 (pbk.), 978-0-316-49541-7 (ebook)

Printed in the United States of America

CW

10 9 8 7 6 5 4 3 2 1

*To the memory of Florence and Richard Atwater and their
children, Doris Atwater and Carroll Atwater Bishop.*

Our grandparents' book, *Mr. Popper's Penguins*, has delighted
children for decades. It has been translated into numerous
languages and has inspired theatrical, musical, and film
adaptations. Now it has inspired a new book, *The Popper
Penguin Rescue*. We hope that you enjoy it.
—Kate and Alec Bishop

Contents

Prologue   Stillwater 1

Chapter 1   Hillport 5

Chapter 2   Nina and Joel Build a Nest 15

Chapter 3   *Oork!* 23

Chapter 4   A Pop Quiz 31

Chapter 5   Ernest and Mae 37

Chapter 6   The Way of All Goldfish 43

Chapter 7   Grounded? 49

Chapter 8   The Popper Foundation 55

Chapter 9   Leaving Hillport 63

Chapter 10   The Journey Begins 69

Chapter 11   Run Aground! 77

Chapter 12   The Popper Penguins 85

Chapter 13   Bleak Prospects 91

Chapter 14   Show and Tell 101

Chapter 15   A Gathering Storm 107

CHAPTER 16   Strange Bedfellows 113

CHAPTER 17   The Huddle 121

CHAPTER 18   A New Destination 125

CHAPTER 19   The Popper Penguins Perform
              an Encore 131

CHAPTER 20   Growing Pains 137

CHAPTER 21   Homecoming 145

CHAPTER 22   Farewell, Dr. Drake 155

STILLWATER

EACH YEAR, STILLWATER held the Popper parade, when everyone would gather to acknowledge the city's most famous residents. Grown-ups took the day off work. No children had to go to classes.

There was good reason to celebrate the Poppers. Mr. Popper had once been an ordinary house painter. But he'd fallen in love with penguins and let his favorite explorer know. Then, one September thirtieth, he'd received a penguin, sent express mail straight from the Antarctic by Admiral Drake himself!

That now-famous penguin, Captain Cook, was soon followed by another, Greta. Once there were a male and female penguin in the house, there were eggs and chicks. The Poppers soon hosted twelve penguins and became very famous after they started up a traveling theatrical act.

From then on, September thirtieth was Stillwater's Popper parade day. The local children would take the bus to school as usual, but they'd cluster in the school-yard instead of going to classes. There, they donned their best penguin costumes, which they had worked hard on in art class. Some looked very accurate. Some looked more like skunks or hamsters.

The adults in the town arrived next, dressed like the Poppers or the other characters from the family's adventure—Mrs. Callahan, Mr. Greenbaum, even Admiral Drake himself! Everyone would have great fun wearing elegant clothes from the 1930s. Then, with the high school marching band blaring away, they all proceeded around town. The kids went first, doing their best impressions of a penguin waddle. The group trundled past the former Popper home at 432 Proudfoot Avenue, past the barber shop and the Palace Theater. The procession finished at the great city square, where news crews came from all over the country to film the merriment.

In the square were copper statues of all twelve Popper Penguins: Captain Cook, Greta, Columbus, Victoria, Nelson, Jenny, Magellan, Adelina, Scott, Isabella, Ferdinand, and Louisa. In the center of those birds were statues of the Poppers and their children. It made quite an image for the front pages of the nation's newspapers. Confetti and ribbons, penguins and Poppers! It was the highlight of every year in Stillwater.

Across the river, in Hillport, it was quite a different story.

HILLPORT

AFTER PASSING THROUGH the neat boulevards of Stillwater, the moving truck rumbled past the low houses and blinking billboards of Hillport. The town had every kind of penguin attraction imaginable. There were penguin petting zoos, penguin gift shops, even a penguin waterslide. The truck eventually came to a stop in front of a sagging building. Light bulbs traced the words *Penguin Pavilion* out front, but not a single bulb was lit, despite the dark evening. The front door of the broken-down petting zoo was boarded up, and the electricity was shut off.

"We're going to live *here*, Mom?" Joel asked, rubbing the car window with his sleeve so he could see better. He didn't mean his words to sound as negative as they did.

"Is there even any power?" asked his little sister, Nina, from the middle seat of the moving truck.

"I have a call in to the electric company," their mother said. "They'll have it back on as soon as they can. Come on, kids, I need you to be flexible and understanding for a few days."

"Are there really going to be *penguins* living inside?" Nina asked, climbing over Joel so she could press her face against the fogged side window. She wiped it with her hand, but her breath immediately fogged it right back up. Joel could see what had caught her attention. Wood cutouts of penguins wearing overalls danced along the outside of the house. A sign below said, Penguin Visits: $5. (Petting Extra. Market Pricing.)

"No penguins here anymore," their mother said, turning off the truck before rummaging through her bag. Her hand emerged with a battered envelope, which

she shook until a single tarnished key dropped into her palm. "Are you ready to go check out our new home?"

"I wish there really were penguins inside," Nina grumbled. "That would make this move worth it."

Joel rubbed the top of her head. "I hear they're actually smelly and cranky. Maybe it's better that we just see them at the zoo, behind glass."

"They wouldn't be smelly and cranky to *me*," Nina protested. "We'd be friends!"

The kids followed their mother along the house's front path. Fading signs promised PENGUIN FEED: $2 and Penguin Portraits: 4 for $4. "This was a penguin petting zoo," their mother explained. "The owners had hoped to make some money from the crowds that came to Stillwater each year to celebrate the Popper story. It's been a very long time since the original Popper Penguins lived in Stillwater, though, and even fewer people come to Hillport each year. The bank foreclosed the Penguin Pavilion, which is why I was able to afford it."

"And the Popper Penguins are part of your history, too, right?" Joel asked. "Which is why we have Popper as our last name?"

"In a way," she said. "But I'm a very distant relation. I never lived in Stillwater or Hillport, so this is as new to me as it is to you kids."

"What does 'foreclosed' mean?" Nina whispered to Joel, while their mother worked to fit the key into the lock.

"I think it means it was closed four times already," Joel said wisely. "That's what makes it cheap enough for Mom to afford."

The front door creaked open. As soon as it did, Nina raced past, her voice reverberating through the halls. "I call this bedroom. No, wait, I call this one instead! You can have that first one!"

Joel didn't much care which room he got. He hung back near his mother, worried by how drawn she looked. It had been a very long drive through bad weather. "Here, Mom," he said, taking her heavy handbag from her and placing it on top of the mantelpiece. "Should I go start unpacking the truck?"

"We can do all that tomorrow," his mom said. She patted the bandanna she always wore over her hair, spattered with paints from her latest canvas. She was a wonderful painter, though she could never seem to settle on any one subject. Some of the tiredness lifted from her eyes. "Nina has the right idea. Let's go explore the house!"

Then she was off, tracking down Nina. Joel closed the front door, made sure the dead bolt was secure, then ran upstairs to join his mother and sister.

The house might have been cheap, but there was a reason. Its previous owners kept penguins here (which was, of course, awesome), but they had clearly not been into housekeeping. Even in the dim reflected light from the streetlamps outside, Joel could see the grime on the walls, and dust and wrappers piled up in the corners. His mother stood in the middle of a cramped kitchen, already working on the faucet, which was spraying out water. When she saw Joel, she gave a tight smile. "At least we know we have running water! Don't worry, we'll get this place cleaned up in no time."

"I'm sure we will, Mom," Joel said, nodding.

"Okay, this one is definitely my room—no, wait, this one!" Nina yelled from upstairs. "There's so many options!"

"You'd better go pick your own bedroom before your sister takes all of them," Mrs. Popper said.

Joel nodded and headed upstairs.

It was a quick choice. Joel let Nina pick whichever room made her happy and then selected the one next door to make life simple. "Come on, it's late and we've got a long day tomorrow," he said to his little sister. "We should go down and unpack our sheets and tooth-brushes, at least."

Nina bounded down the stairs. "Ooh, look, a basement!"

"Let's go unpack, Nina!" Joel called down into the dark. "We can explore the basement tomorrow."

"You have to see this!" she called up. "Amazing! Wow! Bring a flashlight!"

Grumbling, Joel unclipped the flashlight from his belt (he was always prepared for emergencies) and headed down the creaking stairs. There were signs hanging from the ceiling above each step:

Get ready to pet!
Bundle up!
Penguin Pavilion main attraction!
Come meet penguins just
like Captain Cook and Greta!
Buy your tickets upstairs!

"This must be where they kept the penguins," he called to his sister as he stepped off the stairs and onto the cool, dank floor.

"Yes, definitely!" Nina said. "Let's take a look around."

Joel shone the flashlight around the walls. Ice caps and glaciers were painted on each surface, with rough representations of penguins and polar bears playing together in the distance. "Polar bears live in the Arctic,"

11

he said to Nina, "and penguins are in the *Ant*arctic. Totally different poles. And they definitely wouldn't play together. Or wear these silly Santa hats."

"They're just paintings," Nina said, poking around the edges of the room. "I wish the penguins were still here. I've never met a penguin before."

Joel sniffed. "It still smells like birds. And old fish."

Nina took a big sniff, too. "I like the smell. Come here and shine the light on these gigant-o machines!"

Along one wall were what looked like big air conditioners. "These are probably how they kept the room cold."

"Do you think they turn on?" Nina asked.

"Of course they do. But we don't have any power," Joel replied, crossing his arms. "And we don't need to freeze this room if there are no penguins in it anymore. Electricity is expensive."

Nina disappeared around the back of one of the cooling devices. "There's a space back here. I can almost fit—wait, what's that? Whoa, I almost crushed it!"

"Crushed what?" Joel asked, shining the flashlight on his sister. He couldn't see what she'd found, though. Her body was casting a shadow over it.

"Hold on—there's another one!" Nina turned around, with something in each hand.

"What are those?" Joel asked.

She worked her way out from behind the coolers. She was speechless as she lifted her hands up into the light.

It was very unusual for Nina to be speechless.

But in an instant, Joel could see why.

Cradled in each hand was an egg. They were grayish and faintly speckled and too big to be chicken eggs.

They had to be penguin eggs.

NINA AND JOEL BUILD A NEST

"KIDS?" MRS. POPPER asked from the top of the basement stairs. "What's going on down there?"

"Nothing!" Joel called up brightly. He whispered furiously in Nina's ear. "Put those eggs back."

"Why?" Nina protested. "We're going to love these eggs and maybe sit on them and hatch them, and then we'll have penguins!"

"Mom has enough to trouble her without also worrying about the penguin eggs in our basement," Joel whispered.

"Are you kidding? Mom will be excited, too! She loves animals."

"She might make us send them off to whatever zoo the Penguin Pavilion birds wound up in," Joel said. "We wouldn't want that, would we?"

That quieted Nina down. She shook her head soberly.

To be honest, Joel wasn't sure what they should do next. He just knew he didn't like any unexpected complications in his life, and this was definitely an unexpected complication. At least these penguin eggs would probably never hatch. In any case, a few more hours in a corner of the basement wouldn't change their fate. He'd debate about what they should do overnight and then come up with a plan in the morning when he was thinking more clearly.

"Kids?" their mom called down. "Is everything okay?"

"Yes, fine!" Nina called as she carefully returned the eggs to their hiding place. She gave Joel a thumbs-up and winked. Only she hadn't really learned how to wink yet, so it was more like an exaggerated eye scrunch.

Joel didn't sleep much that night. He lay in his strange new bed, looking out at the orange streetlight that shone through the broken slatted blinds of his room, and considered his options.

By morning, he was pretty sure he had a workable plan.

At breakfast, he and Nina sat in a corner of the kitchen, cereal bowls in their laps (they hadn't unpacked any tables and chairs yet). Their mother was in the bathroom, trying to unclog the toilet. It wasn't going well—they kept hearing grunts and strange gurgling sounds. Joel didn't dare peek into the bathroom to see what was going on.

Gloop. Joel coughed. "Mom, Nina and I have to go to our new school on Monday, as you, um, as you know, of course, but did you know they sent a letter to our old house about what we needed to read for class?" *Glork.* "Well, they did, and I memorized it, so, um, I was wondering if Nina and I could go to the library we passed on the way in and get out the books we need. It's just a couple of blocks, and we'll be right back, you'll barely miss us? I'm sure the librarian will be nice and give us a card." *Glup.*

"Sure," their mother called absently. *Glip.* "You're old enough. I'll have this fixed by the time you're back." *Glook.*

Joel and Nina were already halfway out the front

door, pulling their shoes and jackets on. They dressed as they ran, hopping until they had all four shoes on all four feet. "We're looking up how to care for penguin eggs, aren't we?" Nina said excitedly.

Joel nodded and held open the library door for his sister. Once they were inside, Joel and Nina went straight back to the reference section, avoiding the curious gaze of the librarian. They didn't want anyone asking difficult questions.

"Penguins are 598.47," Joel said. "I hope that's a low shelf."

"How do you know the Dewey Decimal number for penguins?" Nina asked.

"I remember stuff, I don't know," Joel said. "Here we go!"

Joel sat on the floor, legs crossed, and pulled books into his lap. "Okay, eggs in the index, page twelve, here we go. Incubation temperature is 96.5 degrees."

"That's really hot, right?" Nina asked.

Joel nodded. "It's been a hot September, but not that hot. We need to get those eggs some heat. I hope it's not too late."

"There was probably heat coming out the back of

the machines, back when power was on," Nina said. She flipped open her own penguin book and sounded out the captions under the photographs. " 'The parents take turns in…in…incubating the eggs.' I guess the little chicks inside like the feeling of being sat on. We should sit on them, too."

Joel snapped his fingers. "Hot-water bottles! We have some from when we were sick last winter."

" 'Sometimes penguin parents wind up being two boys or two girls,' " Nina read out loud. " 'Other penguins will adopt eggs if the original parent goes missing.' That's so sweet."

"Anything else? We should get back and warm those eggs. I wish we could bring the books with us, but of course they won't give library cards to kids without an adult present."

"I don't know why Mom didn't think of that," Nina said.

"She's an *artiste*," Joel replied. "That means she doesn't bother about small things." Like having the power turned on before they arrived at their new home.

Joel started reshelving the books. "Get your coat on, Nina."

"I didn't even take mine off!" Nina said.

"Oh," Joel said, patting his chest, "I didn't, either!"

Back at the house, Joel rushed into the kitchen, while Nina went to rummage the hot-water bottles out of the moving truck. "How's the toilet going, Mom?" Joel called.

"Good!" she replied from the bathroom. "All unclogged. I took a moment to set up the goldfish tank, and now I'm working on the shower drain."

"Great. Say, I'm going to heat water…um, for tea. Do you want some?"

Mrs. Popper ducked into the kitchen, wiping her

brow, a confused expression on her face. "You're making *tea*? Since when have you liked tea?"

"Yeah, um, I heard all the kids here in Hillport and Stillwater like tea. So I thought I'd try it out. I'd have something to talk about in the cafeteria, you know, to make myself some friends on my first day."

"Aww, honey," his mom said, coming over to give him a hug. "You'll make friends in no time. I'm sure of it. You're just the loveliest boy."

"So how does this work?" Joel asked, fiddling with the knobs on the stove top.

"It's gas, which luckily wasn't shut off," his mother said. "Here." The stove top clicked, and blue flames came out of a burner.

"Wow, fire," Joel said. "Let's make lots of hot water, because I want, um, lots and lots of tea!"

"Okay, okay," his mother said distractedly, filling a kettle with water from the sink. "After you drink your tea and do your reading for Monday, I'll need your and your sister's help. I want to give that front hall a good scrub."

"Sounds good," Joel said, staring at the beads of water forming on the sides of the kettle.

Right then Nina came through the front door, an empty hot-water bottle in either hand. "Got 'em!"

"What did you unpack those for?" their mother asked.

"I just like the comforting feel," Nina replied, pressing the rubber against her cheek.

Mrs. Popper narrowed her eyes.

"You know," Joel added hastily, "must be new-school jitters."

"You poor kids," their mother said. "This will be the last new school you ever have to go to, I promise."

"I can handle heating the water from here," Joel said. "Then we'll go do our reading."

"I want to do my reading in the basement!" Nina said.

Joel nodded rapidly. "That's a great idea, Nina."

"Are you kids sure you're okay?" their mother asked, pressing her hand against Joel's forehead.

Nina bounded down the steps into the basement. "Yep, totally! We're great! See you down here once you're ready, Joel!"

"Study hall is in session!" Joel said a few minutes later as he raced down after her with two hot-water bottles in hand. He hoped they wouldn't be too late.

OORK!

IT WAS THEIR first day of school, and Joel and Nina were taking a very long time getting their book bags ready. There were the usual folders and pencil cases and notebooks to color-code and arrange, of course, but there were also secret extra items: fleece blankets, hot-water bottles, and penguin eggs, one for each backpack.

"What's taking you kids so long?" their mother

asked from the front doorway. "You don't want to be late on your first day!"

Joel and Nina gingerly noodled their arms into their shoulder straps, one at a time. "Gently, gently," Joel said as they tiptoed toward the front door.

"What is wrong with you two?" their mother asked, concern on her face as her children crept toward her.

"Oh, you know, first-day jitters," Nina said.

"My dear little ones," Mrs. Popper said. "You'll have friends in no time. I'll walk you there and make sure you get in okay, too."

"No, thanks, Mom," Joel said quickly. "It's only a few blocks away. You took us on that practice run last night. We'll be fine."

"Okay then," she replied, her expression turning wistful. "I'll be right here once the school day's over. I'll want to hear every detail."

"Sounds good, bye, Mom!" Joel said as he and Nina tiptoed out the door. Their mother raised an eyebrow at them, then they were on the sidewalk.

Did Joel feel a nudge inside his backpack? Was that possible?

After arriving at school, they parted ways to go to

their separate homerooms, Joel to fifth grade and Nina to third. Joel moved so carefully through the hallways that he was the last kid to arrive in his room. After greeting him, Mrs. Mosedale placed him in the back row. "I'm seating you next to Michael," she said. "He'll be your guide for the day. Michael, you'll take good care of our new classmate, won't you?"

"Of course I will," Michael said, his face beaming a little too much. He patted Joel on the shoulder, as if they were already friends. "I'll make sure our new buddy knows exactly where he belongs."

For some reason, Joel didn't get a good feeling about Michael. Not at all.

The day started with math, and while Mrs. Mosedale demonstrated how to multiply decimals, Joel's mind wandered. How were Nina and her egg faring in her class? Then he started thinking about the penguin egg in his own backpack. He'd checked on it all weekend. It was almost killing him now not to be able to look at it.

"Mrs. Mosedale?" he asked, raising his hand once she'd assigned them a set of exercises. "Could I go use the bathroom?"

"Of course. Take the hall pass," she said. "Michael, please show Joel the way."

"Sure, Mrs. Mosedale!" Michael said, beaming again. "I'll take him right there." His brightness felt cold, like a fluorescent bulb.

Joel gripped the straps of his backpack and stood.

"You don't need to bring your bag to the bathroom, new kid," Michael said sharply.

"I'd like to," Joel said, and hurried out of the classroom.

"You're weird," Michael said flatly as soon as the door closed. "No one brings their bag to the bathroom."

"I do," Joel said.

"Okay, whatever," Michael said. "The bathroom is down that hall. I'll wait here. I'm not going in with you." Joel could feel Michael's eyes against his back as he cautiously made his way down the hallway.

As soon as he was in the bathroom, Joel dipped into a stall and opened the backpack. The egg was still there, nestled safely in a fleece blanket and warmed by the hot-water bottle. He pulled the egg out. It was so *perfect*. He knew from his reading that its shape made it almost indestructible, even though it was protected by only a thin layer of calcium. It could survive the worst storms of Antarctica yet could also be opened from the inside by a weak baby chick. How amazing!

He flushed the toilet, even though he hadn't done anything. Egg in his hand, he opened the stall door—and ran right into Michael.

"What is that?" Michael said, blocking the exit. "Give it to me, I want to see."

"No way," Joel said.

Joel went to put the egg back in the backpack, but before he could, Michael snatched it from his hands. "What is this? Is it from a dinosaur or something?"

"Give it back!" Joel said, lunging for it.

"No way. This is *awesome*. Everyone's going to love it!" Michael said. With that, he turned and ran.

"No, you'll hurt it! And it needs to stay warm!" Joel cried as he ran after Michael. The thought of the poor baby chick jostling inside, a defenseless little animal that had already been through so much, brought tears to his eyes. Joel ran out of the bathroom and down the hallway.

Michael was *fast*. It was all Joel could do to keep him in view as he raced down the school's unfamiliar corridors. Startled kids peered out of the windows of the classrooms they passed. All it would take was one teacher coming out into the hallway, and it would all be over. The egg would be confiscated.

Michael tossed the egg in the air as he ran, shouting taunts behind him. "You want it back? How much do you want it back?"

"Stop it!" Joel yelled.

Michael slammed through some double doors, and suddenly they were out on the playground, running across the stretch of open asphalt between two basketball hoops. Not too far away, a group of little kids was playing four square. Their teacher was busy taking roll call. No one had noticed the egg—yet.

Michael tossed the egg high in the air and barely caught it, diving for it with both hands extended. Then he tossed the egg right into the air again.

"Give it back!" Joel called as he rushed toward Michael, reaching his arms out to beat him to the falling egg. Like outfielders after a fly ball, they stared up at the sky at the egg turning end over end. It passed in front of the sun, and they were both blinded. The boys knocked into each other. Seeing purple, Joel flailed his hands through the air, hoping to make contact with the egg.

But he didn't. All he heard was a loud crack.

Furious, he shoved Michael away. "No!"

At Joel's feet were ruins of eggshell, gray on the outside and brilliant white on the inside. In the middle was a wet little bird, no bigger than a fist. It was on its side, but then it righted itself and looked directly at Joel. It flapped its miniscule wings, opened and closed its beak. Then it made a sound. *"Oork!"*

A POP QUIZ

NINA'S QUIZ WAS not going well. If only they had started with math, then she would have been right on top of it. Spelling was unfortunately *not* her strong suit. It wasn't fair—she was new, which meant she hadn't had a chance to study any of these words! Mr. Prendergast said just to do her best, and the grade wouldn't count, but even so, Nina took an extra moment to curse being the new kid again. It was the absolute worst.

How did anyone know how to spell *wrinkle*? Nina had an *r* down on her paper, but it already didn't look right.

She spared a moment to glance down at her bag, which she'd left open at the side of her desk—quite cleverly, she thought. She could check on the egg all through class. It was nestled snugly in its fleece blanket, heat radiating up from the hot-water bottle, enough to turn Nina's forehead sweaty.

Wait—did the egg have a crack in it?

"Eyes on your paper, Nina," Mr. Prendergast said.

"Sorry," Nina said, returning to *wrinkle*. Her face flushed even more. He thought she'd been cheating! This was not going to be a good first impression.

"The next word," Mr. Prendergast said, "is 'content,' as in 'satisfied.' 'Content.'"

Nina spent a long time penciling a *c*, sneaking glances at her bag. The egg was definitely shaking, and the crack was getting bigger. She could hear a tapping sound. She scratched her pencil harder along her paper, hoping that sound would cover the ones coming from the egg.

Oh my! There was a *hole* in the egg now, and from the other side of the hole emerged a little beak, hard and black and with a hook on the end. Nina knew from her library research that that was called an egg tooth. The chick was coming out! She wished Joel were here to see. Some situations just called for a big brother.

She had only one letter down again when Mr. Prendergast called out the next word. *Highway.* This one Nina had a better chance on.

She just let her pencil make random movements on the paper, though, while she stared down at the chick. It was fully out of its shell now. A real live baby penguin! Oh my gosh!

Then it made its first noise: A very small *oork!* The student on Nina's right looked up and around, confused.

Uh-oh. This was going to get out of hand very quickly.

"Oork, oork!"

Before Nina could stop it, the chick picked its way out of the shell, then up and out of her backpack and onto the classroom floor. "No, stop!" she whispered as the bird started toddling under her desk, holding out its flippers. It was very cute, a dark gray ball of fuzz with a white belly and sleepy black eyes. But cuteness wouldn't be enough to keep the bird from getting both of them into trouble very quickly.

" 'Nectar,' " Mr. Prendergast called out as the chick gave the leg of Nina's desk an experimental peck.

Nina slunk down in her desk, slipped onto the floor, and got up on her hands and knees.

What are you doing? the girl next to her mouthed.

Nina reached her hands around the chick. It was so fragile and light, bits of egg still stuck to its feathers. The chick disappeared entirely in Nina's hands. It felt like holding a Christmas ornament. Nina eased back into her chair, hands cupping the baby penguin. It pecked at Nina's palms. It tickled.

"Is everything okay, Nina?" Mr. Prendergast asked, looking over at her.

Nina nodded emphatically.

As Mr. Prendergast called out " 'Adapt,' " Nina delicately lowered her hands into her backpack and released the chick. Before it could get out again, she zipped the bag shut.

She could still hear the chick making its squeaky *oork* sounds inside. The girl next to her had given up on her quiz and was staring at Nina's shaking backpack with astonishment. This situation was soon going to... what was the word...

" 'Escalate,' " Mr. Prendergast called.

Yep! That was it!

Nina had just written an *e* down on her paper when Joel appeared at the classroom door. He looked sweaty and out of breath, wearing his backpack on his front. If Nina wasn't mistaken, Joel's bag was shaking, too.

"Can I help you, young man?" asked Mr. Prendergast, clearly irritated at the interruption.

"I'm sorry," Joel said. "My name is Joel Popper. Nina is my sister, and I have to go home sick. Our mother is on the way. The front office said I could come get Nina, so we could go home together."

"Are you sure? That's most unusual," Mr. Prendergast said, folding his arms over his sweater vest.

Nina looked from her brother to Mr. Prendergast, her mind racing. Then she coughed. Her hand was already reaching for her backpack. "Yes, I'm feeling sick, too!"

ERNEST AND MAE

"KIIIIDS," MRS. POPPER said as she walked them home, "are you *sure* that you're both sick?"

"Yes, of course we are," Joel said quickly.

Nina coughed pointedly.

Their mother was carrying their backpacks for them, which she always did when they weren't feeling well. Joel watched the bags to see if the chicks were moving. But they weren't, and he couldn't hear any *oorks*. Maybe the chicks had fallen asleep.

Mrs. Popper chose her words carefully. "I wonder if maybe you two were overwhelmed by your first day, and you called out sick because you wanted to come home."

Nina coughed again, shaking her head at the same time.

Joel always felt terrible whenever he lied, so he took the opportunity to clear his conscience. "Yeah, that might have been it, Mom. We just wanted to come home."

Nina stopped coughing.

"I wish you had told me the truth from the start."

Nina took their mother's hand in hers and squeezed. "Sorry, Mom. They might not have called you if we didn't say we were sick."

Mrs. Popper ruffled Nina's hair. "I know this move is hard on you both. None of us expected your father to leave, that I'd have to find a way to get by on one income. But we have a house we can call ours now. We *own* it. Everything is going to be different from here on out."

"I bet you're right, Mom," Joel said. "That sounds nice."

"I love you two," Mrs. Popper said.

"Do we have any tuna fish?" Joel asked.

"Oh!" Mrs. Popper said, surprised. "We...*do* have tuna fish."

As soon as they were inside, Joel and Nina dashed upstairs and huddled in Nina's room, where they unzipped their backpacks and peered in.

"Oh, thank God," Joel said as he pulled his chick out. It sat on his palm quietly, peering up at him with its deep, dark eyes.

"Mine's okay, too!" Nina cried. Her chick was far more energetic, hopping out of her hand and wandering around the room, checking out the corners, *oork*ing away. Nina sighed. "It's so cute!"

"It is. They both are," Joel said, lowering his chick to the ground. It chased after Nina's, and once it'd caught up, it huddled against the other penguin, little fuzzy wing reaching out for comfort. They both kept *oork*ing. "I bet they're hungry."

"I'll go get the tuna fish," Nina said, and ran downstairs.

Joel kneeled on the floor. Tears of joy filled his eyes while he watched the chicks. They were so perfect. Then he leaped to his feet. The penguins were heading right out of the bedroom! Joel shut the door just in time, before the chicks wandered out into the hallway. They hit the wood and turned around. The startled chicks *oork*ed even louder. Two baby penguins were going to be a lot of work.

"Here, you two," Joel said, lying on his stomach so he was eye level with them. "Come say hi."

The penguins waddled over awkwardly, passing right by Joel's head and wedging into the space between his neck and the floor, one on either side. Joel laughed. "You guys want to feel like you're under an adult penguin's belly, don't you?"

"*Oork! Oork!*"

Fuzzy feathers tickled Joel's throat. It was all he could manage not to laugh out loud.

The door creaked open. Joel didn't want to disturb the nesting penguins, so he didn't dare look up to see who was coming in. He was relieved to see Nina's sneakers coming toward him, not his mother's loafers.

Nina set down a plate of tuna fish. "We're lucky Mom is so distracted by moving in," she said. "She didn't even notice I was making a plate of plain tuna. Come on, birds, it's lunchtime!"

The chicks wriggled out from under Joel's throat. They waddled over to the plate, brought their eyes close to the fish, then looked up at Nina and Joel expectantly.

40

"What are they waiting for?" Joel asked.

"In the books from the library, it looked like the parents fed the chicks."

"I don't remember that part. How do they feed them? It's not like penguins have hands to hold fish."

"No, they . . . you know, re*gurg*itate." Nina opened her mouth and did a very believable impression of vomiting.

"Gross."

Nina picked up a piece of tuna and dangled it over the chicks' heads. They opened their mouths and bounced. *"Oork! Oork!"* She dropped the morsel into one mouth, and the chick happily gummed it down.

Joel sat up, selected a piece of tuna, and dropped it into the other chick's mouth. That bird, too, eagerly swallowed the food.

"We should call them Hungry and Eat-y," Nina proposed.

"The Popper Penguins were named after famous travelers," Joel said. "We don't know if these are boys or girls yet, but what if we named them Ernest, for Ernest Shackleton, who went to the South Pole, and . . . and—"

"Mae, for Mae Jemison!" Nina said. "She went to space."

"Perfect."

"That'll be the more energetic one. Your shyer one can be Ernest."

Joel picked Ernest up and looked into his eyes. "You can be as shy as you want. We'll take good care of you."

"Kids!" their mother called from downstairs. "You promised to help me, since you're not actually sick!"

"We'll take these two down to the basement and then go help Mom," Joel whispered.

They each scooped a chick into their T-shirts and hustled downstairs.

They opened the basement door—which squeaked. "Kids, now! I'm not messing around," their mom called.

"Sorry, Mom!" They deposited the chicks, their fleece blankets, hot-water bottles, and tuna fish in the middle of the basement floor, then raced upstairs.

As Joel closed the basement door, all he could hear were the bewildered *oork*s of the chicks.

"I don't think we'll be able to pull this off for too long," Nina whispered to Joel as they rushed toward their mother.

"I don't know if we'll be able to pull it off for a *day*," Joel replied.

It would turn out to be closer to ten minutes.

THE WAY OF ALL GOLDFISH

THE FIRST TASK of the day was to finish unloading the moving truck so their mother could return it. Each time Joel went to get a box, he tried to pick one that was labeled BASEMENT, so he could check on Ernest and Mae. But Mrs. Popper wasn't playing along. "We should save the basement boxes for the end, kids. That's the last priority. Start with the bedroom stuff, so we can get this house feeling like a home."

"If only she knew," Nina said under her breath as she dragged a floor lamp through the front door, passing right under the old PENGUIN PAVILION sign.

Joel put his hands on his hips and looked around the moving truck. "Mom, where'd you wind up putting the goldfish?"

"Winkles and Joffrey?" she said, wiping her brow. "I think it might have been the basement."

Joel nearly dropped the box he was holding. "You put them in the basement?" He ran out of the truck and into the house. "Nina! The goldfish are in the basement!"

"So what?" Nina said. Then she saw Joel's horrified expression. "Oh! The basement!"

They threw open the door and ran down the steps.

They were just in time to see the goldfishes' tails disappear down the penguin's open beaks, one in each. *Slurp, slurp.*

"Oork, oork!"

The chicks waddled forward and back, turning in circles and raising their little wings, clearly pleased with themselves.

Nina stood openmouthed. "Goodbye, Winkles."

Joel put his arm around her shoulders. "Goodbye, Joffrey."

Emboldened, Mae hopped up onto the first step and then the second. Ernest looked at Mae in wonderment, then tried to hop onto the first step. It didn't go nearly as well. He hit the step mid-belly and then fell back to the floor, astonished. *"Oork! Oork!"* he cried.

Joel rushed to cradle him, while Nina played defense, positioning her feet along a step to prevent Mae from jumping any higher, looking just like a soccer goalie trying to block a shot.

Mae might have been only a few hours old, but she was already clever. She waddled left on her step and then took a surprise waddle to the right before jumping, skirting right by Nina.

Then Mae was up and out of the basement door and into the rest of the house.

"Oh no, oh no," Nina cried as she scrambled after the fast-moving chick.

The baby penguin was already in the kitchen, pecking at the corner of a cardboard moving box, when Nina caught up to her. She scooped up the cuddly little chick. "You have to stay in the basement, naughty Mae!"

Nina heard a loud gasp. She turned and nearly dropped the chick in surprise.

There, mouth open in a wide O of astonishment, was Mrs. Popper.

GROUNDED?

IT WAS A very somber family meeting. Or it would have been a very somber family meeting, if two penguin chicks hadn't been wandering around the dining room table. Mae and Ernest *oork*ed with curiosity, frequently lifting their wings up and down until someone cuddled them.

"I cannot *believe* that you kids thought it was okay to lie to me," Mrs. Popper was saying. She had to break off, though, when Ernest stood in front of her and fixed her with an intense stare. "What do *you* want?"

"He wants you to hold him," Joel explained.

Mrs. Popper nervously picked up the chick and cradled him in the crook of her elbow. Her expression melted. "Is that better, Ernest? Anyway, what was I saying, oh, right, I'm very mad at you for thinking you could lie to your very own mother—what do you want? Are you hungry, little Ernest? Aww!"

"They really love tuna fish," Nina said quietly.

"Well, we should stock up," Mrs. Popper said. "We have only a couple of cans left." She struggled to turn her expression stern again. "This doesn't mean that I'm okay with your lying to me. You two are still in big trouble."

Joel nodded solemnly. "Yes. Big trouble. Got it."

"We didn't want you to send them to the zoo!" Nina wailed.

"We think they should live with *us*," Joel clarified.

"They can*not* live with us," Mrs. Popper said. "That's not negotiable. Penguins do not belong in houses."

"The Poppers did it!" Nina said.

"That was a long time ago," Mrs. Popper said. "And

what happened in the end? They realized that the penguins needed to be in nature, and Mr. Popper did the right thing. He brought them back to the wild."

"Mom?" Joel said.

"Yes, Joel?"

"The Penguin Pavilion was already closed when we got here, so I didn't see it in action or anything, but I don't think it sounds like it was a good place for penguins. They left two eggs behind! I don't think they deserve to have Ernest and Mae back."

Their mother sighed. "I'm inclined to agree. Also, I don't know where they are. The Penguin Pavilion left in the middle of the night, without telling anyone where they were going. They owed a lot of money and just disappeared."

Through with cuddles for the moment, Ernest thrashed until Mrs. Popper released him onto the table. He waddled over to the edge and sniffed the air, beak pointing toward the kitchen. He had clearly decided it was time to eat again. As if to make a point, he deposited a bright white smear of penguin poo on the tabletop.

"I'll clean that up!" Joel said hurriedly.

As a parent, Mrs. Popper found a smear of poo was

no big deal. Without missing a beat, she pulled a hand-kerchief out of her back pocket and wiped it away.

"Does that mean we're *not* bringing them to the zoo? But you also said they couldn't stay here. I guess I'm confused," Nina said.

"I'm a little confused, too," Mrs. Popper confessed. She'd always been very honest with her children. "These penguins belong in the wild, but we can't exactly bring them to the local beach, can we? They need a *cold* wilderness."

Joel thought for a long moment. "Every kid around here knows that Mr. Popper brought his penguins up to the Arctic, to Popper Island," he said. "What if we brought these chicks up to live with them?"

Nina hooted. "That would be amazing!"

Never one to be left out, Mae gave an excited *oork* from where she was nestled in Nina's arms.

"It's fall break soon," Nina said, petting Mae's fuzzy head. "We could go then!"

"Just how do you kids imagine we'll get all the way to the Arctic?" Mrs. Popper asked.

"Stillwater might be the fancier city," Joel said, "but

there's one advantage to living in Hill*port*, if you catch my drift."

"I have no idea what you're talking about," Nina said.

"Port, Nina, *port*," he said, pantomiming a ship rocking on the sea.

"Oh, yay!" Nina said. "I do like traveling by boat!"

THE POPPER FOUNDATION

IT WAS ONLY their second day of school, and yet the Popper children had already accomplished so much. They'd hatched two penguin chicks and come up with a plan for how to find them a home. Nina had even learned her spelling words—she wasn't going to repeat *that* disaster again!

While the kids were in school, they left their chicks under the watchful eye of Mrs. Popper. As Ernest and

Mae napped in the morning, Mrs. Popper went to the library to do some research of her own. She soon discovered that hatched birds don't need any special heat sources in a temperate climate like Hillport's—in fact their feathers insulated them so well that, until winter came, they'd need a way to cool down!

She went to the grocery store and bought some big bags of ice, which she dumped into a shallow tub in the corner of the kitchen. The penguins were smart creatures, she figured, and could decide how cold they wanted to be, using the ice as much as they saw fit. And that's just what they did, hopping into the tub to play in the cubes for a while before joining Mrs. Popper in unpacking dishes (a task at which they were distinctly unhelpful), and then returning to the ice bath for some more cooling down.

As soon as the school day was over, the kids bounded home to see their chicks. Ernest and Mae greeted them with many cheeps and *oork*s. First the kids brought the chicks to the bathtub to swim laps. Then Joel lay on the floor, belly-down, and Ernest happily burrowed under his throat, his nesting position. Nina and Mae did the same. "Could you get our schoolbags for us, Mom?"

Nina asked. "We'd better get used to doing our home-work in this position."

Mrs. Popper retrieved their bags from where they'd dropped them by the front door. "Once the penguins have had their snuggles and you've all had your afternoon snack, we'll go down to the port to visit the Popper Foundation and see what they can do to help put our plan into action."

"Really?" Joel said. "We're going to ask them to get us to Popper Island? All the way in the Arctic?"

"That will be the best fall break ever," Nina said.

"Can we bring Ernest and Mae to the port with us?" Joel asked once the snack was over.

"It does seem sad to leave them behind," Mrs. Popper said. "Yes, we'll bring them to the Popper Foundation, as long as you kids hold them tight."

Ernest and Mae seemed to enjoy the car trip, turn-ing their heads to and fro so they could peer out with one eye and then the other. Joel was learning that they didn't face what they were looking at, usually, because of where their eyes were placed on their heads. Hav-ing an eye on either side allowed them to see all around them—which was probably very useful for avoiding seals in the water!

Once they'd parked at the harbor, Mrs. Popper led the kids to an address she'd written down on the back of an envelope. It was the office of the Popper Foundation. They knocked on a beautiful wooden door, carved with decorations of twelve regal-looking penguins.

The door buzzed open, and the Poppers filed into the foundation's office.

"Sorry, busy today, come again another time," the foundation representative said without looking up from his desk. He was a blustery bald man, with dried sea salt on his moustache.

Mae cheeped in outrage. The representative looked up. "Oh! Penguins!"

"We have two penguins here that need to get to the wild," Nina said, sticking out her chest a trifle self-importantly. "And we're *Poppers*. Distant relations."

"Penguins!" the representative behind the desk repeated, his face warming at the sight of the two fuzzy little chicks.

"We're hoping that we can bring these two to Popper Island, to live with the Popper Penguins!" Joel said.

"My understanding is that the only way to communicate with Popper Island is by maritime radio," Mrs.

Popper said. "Could you try to ring them up for us, to ask if they might be able to pick these chicks up the next time they come to town for supplies?"

"I'll try," the representative said, cracking his knuckles. "But it won't go well."

They all watched as he put on a headset and turned some dials. Even the chicks went silent, watching curiously from Nina's and Joel's arms. "Popper Island Station come in, Popper Island Station come in." He removed the headset and turned back to them. "No answer. In fact, there's been no answer for months."

"Doesn't that count as an emergency?" Mrs. Popper asked, surprised.

"It's been decades since Mr. Popper brought the original twelve penguins there, of course. The foundation pays a local guy to be the island's caretaker now. There wasn't a distress signal. Perhaps the caretaker left the penguins to run themselves for a few weeks. That's no crisis in my book."

"It could be a crisis for the penguins!" Nina said hotly. "Mr. Popper would be outraged!"

"Won't there be an investigation?" Joel tried.

"I'm afraid there's nothing like that planned," the representative said.

The kids looked up at their mother. She crossed her arms, kneading the elbows of her well-worn jacket. "Is there any other way to get to Popper Island? Someone needs to figure out if everything is okay. And get these two chicks up there."

The representative pulled out an atlas, laid it flat on his desk, and beckoned them all to come around. Joel and Nina placed Mae and Ernest on top of the map. The chicks peered in wonder at the greens and blues beneath their feet.

The man with the mustache pointed at a small blip off the east coast of Canada. "That's Popper Island, see?" As he gestured with his fingers, Mae took a curious nip at his wedding band. The burly representative ignored her as he traced a path along the blue ink of the water. "This is where the fishing routes normally go. As you can see, none of them travel anywhere near."

The kids' faces fell.

"We have to find a way to get there," Mrs. Popper said resolutely.

"Well, yes, madam," the representative said, smiling for the first time that afternoon. "This is the Popper Foundation, and our purpose is to care for the Popper Penguins. We care a great deal." He scrawled a name and phone number down on a piece of paper. "Contact Yuka. He grew up near Popper Island and takes trips back up there sometimes to visit his family. He has a sturdy little boat and is an excellent captain. He'll get your penguins there safely. Of course, the Popper Foundation will fund the expedition, since you'll also be doing us the favor of reporting back on how the Popper birds are doing."

"*Oork!*" said Mae triumphantly, before taking another friendly nip at the representative's knuckle.

LEAVING HILLPORT

THE SMALL BOAT dipped and rocked where it was tied to the Hillport dock. "Are you sure this is seaworthy? I mean, *Arctic* seaworthy?" Joel whispered to his mother.

"This looks amazing!" Nina said, bounding aboard. She held Mae out in her palms, turning in a circle. The chick peered up and down. *"Oork, oork!"* In just the last few weeks, her voice had changed some. Her *oork*s were getting closer to adult penguin *ork*s.

"It's going to be totally safe," Mrs. Popper said as she stepped onto the deck. "Come on, kids, I want to introduce you to Yuka."

Joel and Nina brought their two chicks to Yuka. He was a young man with an open, friendly face.

"Hi there!" Yuka said. When he reached out his hand for a shake, Joel didn't know what to do at first and gave him his left hand, until he realized he should switch them, awkwardly juggling Ernest in the process. Nina, of course, figured out handshakes right away.

"Yuka is Inuit," Mrs. Popper explained. "That means

his ancestors lived in the Arctic long before Europeans got there."

Yuka nodded. "It's been a few years since I lived up there, though. I came down to Stillwater College to get my doctorate in comparative zoology. I study aquatic bird migrations, actually! That's why the Popper Foundation knew about me."

Ernest made an impressed *oork*. Joel was more suspicious. "So you're not actually a sailor?"

"I come from a long line of fishermen. This is my family's boat. It's a wonderful deep-sea fishing vessel and does fine in rough waters. Don't worry—I know how to handle the waterways. And I have a seminar paper due in a few weeks, so I'll make sure this is an efficient trip. You won't miss any school, and neither will I!"

"It's not like missing school would be *that* terrible," Nina said.

"We're very grateful, Yuka," Mrs. Popper said. "Thank you for taking this time."

"It's an honor to help these little guys," Yuka said. He ducked his head to get a better look at the fuzzy gray chicks. "I like those pretty white stripes on your flippers!"

"*Oork! Oork!*" Ernest turned around so Yuka could see his coloring on all sides. He was turning out to be a vain little penguin.

Yuka tilted his head at Mrs. Popper. "You've got everything from the packing list we settled on?"

"Yes! Lots of warm, waterproof layers."

"And tuna fish!" Nina added.

"That's good," Yuka said. "This boat may still smell a little like fish, but it's been years since it did any fishing. I just use it to get back and forth to school. So it's good you're bringing your own food for the birds." He threw open the small hatch that led belowdecks. "Here are our quarters. Not too roomy, but I've always liked it down there. 'Homey' is probably the best word for it."

Joel peeked in. The cabin was clean and pleasant, with a fridge and a small stove top and neatly made bunks covered in red plaid sheets. A fine place to spend a week.

"I think we're ready to go!" Mrs. Popper said.

"All aboard!" Yuka called. He leaned down to confide in Joel. "I've always wanted to say that, but it would feel silly when I'm traveling alone."

Once the boat had been freed from the dock, Yuka started the engine. Before long, they were puttering out of Hillport harbor.

The kids placed their chicks on the deck. The penguins waddled over to the edge, to gaze down at the water flowing past the boat. They'd taken to swimming laps in the bathtub, so Joel wasn't too worried about what would happen if they fell in. Yuka would just stop the boat and fish them out of the water. The chicks would be sure to enjoy the process immensely.

"Once we get up there," Nina whispered, "how are we going to say goodbye to Ernest and Mae?"

"We'll find a way," Joel said, putting an arm around his sister. "Being with other penguins is what's right for them."

Nina kneeled at the edge of the deck. Mae toddled over and hopped into her lap. "I guess. But it'll still be hard to say goodbye."

Not one to be left out, Ernest pinched the fabric of Nina's jeans with his beak and lifted himself into her lap. He was turning out to be a smaller penguin than his sister and sometimes needed help getting himself everywhere he wanted to go.

"I know it will be hard," Joel said, watching Ernest snuggle in closer to Nina. "I know it."

Ernest let out a long *oooork*. "Sounds like he knows it, too," Nina said.

"Actually, I think that just means he's ready for some more tuna fish."

THE JOURNEY BEGINS

JOEL LOVED SPENDING his day at the helm with Yuka. There were so many instruments and panels to investigate, and Yuka would often let him take control—while keeping an eye out, of course.

Sometimes Joel would catch his mother watching the two of them with an expression that looked both sad and happy. It wasn't hard to imagine where her thoughts were. Joel sometimes overheard his mother talking to her friends on her phone about how she was worried Joel didn't have any "male role models" in his life. But that was ridiculous. Joel wasn't excited to spend time with Yuka because he was a "male role model." It was all about the instruments and panels!

Nina would often want her turn, too, so they'd switch off, and Joel would take over minding the chicks. Mae and Ernest spent most of each day sleeping. At first Joel and Nina had been worried they were sick, but then Mrs. Popper pointed out that the chicks were probably sleeping so much because they were growing so fast.

Apparently Joel and Nina had done the same thing when they were babies.

When the chicks weren't sleeping, they made plenty of trouble. Ernest preferred to be at the stern. Sometimes he'd poke around the boat's engines, investigating the various humming devices. Other times he'd stare into the waves and flap his wings—Joel could imagine him preparing for the day when he'd be swimming through ocean water. Mae preferred to be perched at the bow, like the figurehead on a pirate ship. Whichever kid was on duty would have to walk the deck, making sure that neither chick fell into the surf.

Chicks falling overboard wouldn't turn out to be the problem.

Yuka was an excellent sailor, diligently minding the controls even as he told elaborate tales about his childhood in the Arctic, complete with impersonations of all his family members. On the fourth morning, though, he seemed preoccupied. He spent a long time examining his atlas after he pulled up anchor.

"This makes no sense," he said.

Mrs. Popper, Joel, and Nina crowded around Yuka. Not to be left out, Ernest and Mae *oork*ed until the kids picked them up so they could see what all the fuss was about.

"All my instrumentation agrees that we're here," Yuka said, pointing to a spot on the map as the boat sped forward.

"That's good, right?" Nina said.

"Yes," Yuka said, drawing out the word as he pointed at the horizon. "But if that's true, we wouldn't be here already."

"We wouldn't be *where* already?" Joel asked.

"Popper Island!"

"What?" Nina yelled, jumping up and down.

"Careful with Mae," Joel scolded. But the chick was clearly enjoying the action, her cries joining Nina's. Joel put a hand over his eyes, like a visor, and squinted. They were approaching a windswept pile of dark gray rocks, sticking up out of the ocean. It looked brutal and unforgiving to Joel—but who knew, maybe it was paradise to a penguin's eyes.

"Are you sure that's Popper Island ahead of us?" Mrs. Popper asked.

Yuka nodded. "Definitely. I grew up around here, and I'd recognize those rock formations anywhere."

"But how could all your instruments be wrong?" Nina asked.

"They're connected to a central computer on the boat," Yuka said. "If my navigation systems have us in the wrong position it really isn't good, because that means I don't have readouts on nearby undersea obstacles. It's dangerous."

"Where is the computer located?" Joel asked with a sinking feeling.

"At the stern."

Joel slipped away to the back of the boat, Ernest chirping happily once he realized they were heading to his favorite spot. He hopped down and examined the engine like usual before sitting and gazing into the water.

Joel spied the computer, housed in a plastic box on the floor. He'd never bothered to look closely at it before. A corner had been bent away, the contents dragged out onto the deck. Some wires, some transistors, some microchips. Right in front of Joel's eyes, Ernest reached in with his beak, pulled out another microchip, toddled to the edge of the boat, and pitched it over. He watched happily as it dropped into the rushing waves, then looked up at Joel with pride. *"Oork!"*

"Oh no!" Joel yelled, hands on his cheeks. "Yuka, Ernest's been meddling with the computer!"

There was no answer from the helm. Joel ran up there to find Yuka gripping the wheel with white knuckles, Mrs. Popper and Nina standing beside him. "What's going—"

"There!" Yuka shouted, pointing at a dark shape in the water, passing under the prow. "That's the rocks—hold on tight!"

Joel was interrupted by a horrible grinding sound from the hull. The whole vessel slowed, and the bow dipped, pitching them all forward. They barely caught themselves at the railing, Mae tight in Nina's hand, narrowly missing getting pinned against the rail.

At first it felt like the boat might tip over and cast them into the sea. The back rose alarmingly, then crashed back into the ocean. The engines continued to roar, but the boat didn't move forward anymore. It just ground against the undersea rocks.

While Yuka frantically manned the helm, throwing levers and pushing buttons to cut the engines before the boat tore itself apart, Joel raced to the stern. He could just imagine Ernest cast into the sea, falling toward the propeller blades below. "Ernest!"

The chick was toddling toward him. Joel scooped him up, relieved. As he did, though, the boat listed to one side. Crates of food supplies tumbled into the waves.

"Everyone to shore!" Yuka shouted from the helm. "We've run aground!"

RUN AGROUND!

JOEL AND NINA and Mrs. Popper crouched at the edge of the tilting boat, staring into the turbulent gray-black water between them and the icy shore. Even though they had huddled together, they were shivering. The arctic wind cut between the fibers of their coats and ripped the heat away from their bodies. The prospect of being wet on top of being so cold was not appealing at all.

"Now, kids, wait until I've gone across, then I'll help you," Mrs. Popper said. Her words were brave, but she didn't look ready to cross the slanting gangway to the slippery rocks, not at all.

Mae, nestled in Nina's mittens, took one look up at her...and then leaped right into the sea!

"Mae, no!" Nina called. But Mae transformed once she hit the water, turning from awkward puffball to sleek missile. She arrowed through the surf, then sprang out with such force that she landed a few yards onto the rocky land, rolling and rolling before she got to her feet.

Ernest joined her, arrowing through the water just as capably—only he unfortunately landed in the very same spot as Mae, bowling her over and sending them both tumbling across the ground, squawking all the while. They got to their feet and stared at their human companions expectantly. *Come on, this is fun!*

"I think the tables are turning," Joel said. "The moment we cross over this water, *they're* the ones who are in their element, and we're the outsiders."

Mrs. Popper went first, just managing to keep her footing and make it to the island, staggering in her heavy fur-lined boots. Nina was next, using her mother's outstretched arm to steady herself. Finally came Joel, helped by both his sister and mother.

"We did it, Yuka!" Mrs. Popper called back toward the boat.

Yuka looked up from the engine, pulling a metal mask back from his face. His welding tool continued to spark as he cheered and waved. "That's great! The caretaker's hut is on the far side of the island. I'll come join you as soon as I know there's no more water coming in."

"Are you sure you don't want to come now?" Joel called. He would miss having Yuka nearby, the zany stories he told and his cheerful outlook on life and all his knowledge of gizmos and gadgets. Life felt safer when he was around.

"We definitely don't want to anchor a leaking boat, or we'll have an even bigger crisis on our hands," Yuka said. "I want to get us all back home before your break's over and my paper's due!"

"He's very dedicated, isn't he?" Mrs. Popper said. "The Popper Foundation put us in good hands."

"We'll come report back on what we discover!" Nina called, skipping ahead across the rocks.

Joel shivered and rubbed his arms. "Let's go find that hut."

"Maybe there are s'mores there!" Nina called over her shoulder.

Mrs. Popper nibbled on the thumb of her mitten, a sure sign she was worried. "I don't think there are going to be any s'mores there, sweetie. Don't get your hopes up."

Joel gave her arm a rub. "Don't worry, Mom. This is going to be okay."

"I should be comforting *you*," she said.

"And we should be comforting *them*," Joel said. "But that's not how it's working out." He pointed ahead, where Mae and Ernest were waddling their way along the barren ground, getting right back up each time they fell down—which was often—on the island's icy rocks.

Nina led the charge, scrambling to catch up to the little penguin chicks. The Poppers were out of breath by the time they reached them. Together the group crested a rise so they could take in the whole of the island.

It was rocky and treeless, a mountaintop surrounded by frigid seas. Boulders rose in strange formations, making much of the island impassable. The sides of all the stones were streaked in white—maybe penguin poo, maybe from other seabirds.

"Where *are* the Popper Penguins?" Joel asked.

"The hut is on the north of the island, on the other side of those big boulders," Mrs. Popper said. "It's next to the beach, where boats are *supposed* to land if they don't want to hit rocks and get big holes gashed into them."

"A beach!" Nina said, clapping her hands. "That sounds great."

"A very cold beach," Joel added soberly. He knew his sister's mind had probably gone right to sunblock and sandcastles.

They picked their way along the rocks. Joel tried to carry Ernest as they went, but the penguin made an *oork* of outrage and nipped Joel's finger. Apparently the chicks preferred to travel on their own two feet now that they were in their sort of environment.

As the Poppers made their way around a final sharp outcropping of rock, the caretaker's hut came into view.

It was a teetering brown shack, its planks warped and darkened by sea air. A few of its shingles were loose, clapping against the frame.

"It doesn't seem like anyone is home," Joel said.

"No, it definitely doesn't appear that way," Mrs. Popper said.

"Would you look at that?" Joel said, pointing above the front door as they approached.

"What? I can't see!" Nina said, jumping up and down.

Mrs. Popper picked Nina up and held her high enough so she could read. Nina took her time, sounding out the words. "Here marks the hut built by Mr. Popper and Admiral Drake, the two gentlemen who brought penguins to the Arctic. Nineteen hundred and thirty-six."

"Mr. Popper was actually *here*!" Joel said. "That's so cool."

Once they'd made their way inside, they found a cabinet with cans of food, a gas stove, a simple sort of ship's radio, and a sleeping platform with woolen blankets.

"Those men weren't into luxuries, were they?" Mrs. Popper said.

"They were *explorers*," Nina said indignantly. "Of course they weren't into luxuries."

"It does seem like they could at least have put in a reading lamp," Mrs. Popper said.

"Let's get this place heated up," Joel said as he worked on latching the door closed.

"Look, a piece of paper," Nina said, after rummaging around under the bed. "Something's written on it!"

"Read it out loud," Mrs. Popper said as she did an inventory of the canned foods.

"You can do it this time," Nina said, thrusting the paper at her brother.

Joel cleared his throat. "'To whomever it may concern: Please forgive my leaving my post. I developed a toothache that's making it impossible to monitor the Popper Penguins for the time being. I will return as soon as it's fixed and I've had a chance to see my family.'"

"That's it?" Nina asked.

"Yep," Joel said, after turning the paper over to check.

"When is it dated?" Mrs. Popper asked.

"Um...a month ago."

"Is that long enough for..." Mrs. Popper let her words trail off.

"Long enough for what?" Joel asked.

"It's just that...that there's no sign of the Popper Penguins. Could something have happened to them after the caretaker left?"

"Oh no!" Nina said, clutching Mae close to her.

"Oh no, indeed." Mrs. Popper sighed as she looked through the cabinets. "Aside from the state of the Popper Penguins, we have something else to worry about. There's only about three days' worth of food here."

"But Yuka needs more time than that to repair the boat," Joel said.

"Wait, what does that mean?" Nina asked.

Joel shook his head and buried his face in Ernest's soft side. "It means we're in big trouble."

Which was precisely when they heard a chorus of *ork*s from the beach outside the hut.

THE POPPER PENGUINS

THERE WERE PENGUINS outside the caretaker's hut. Many, many penguins. They milled about, staring at the hut and swaying back and forth, making a raucous chorus of *ork*s and *jook*s and *gaw*s. One by one they stepped forward, turned in a circle, then returned to the group. It looked like some kind of welcome dance.

"Are those...the Popper Penguins?" Nina asked.

"I think so," Joel said. "You remember the penguin

statues in Stillwater? These look just like them. They have the same white lines on their cheeks that the Popper Penguins had, too."

"There's a lot more than twelve of these, though!" Mrs. Popper exclaimed.

Penguins kept arriving. They emerged from the surf, springing onto land just like Mae and Ernest had. They were confident as they sped through the water but became nervous and hesitant as soon as they were on the shore, scanning around to see what their friends were doing before they committed to walking up onto the beach.

There they each did their turnabout dance before huddling into the group, craning around one another to get the best view of the hut and the people emerging from it.

"Hello there," Mrs. Popper said, raising her hand in greeting.

"*Ork! Ork! Ork!*" The penguins fell back in fear, one bumping into the next until they all pitched over like a set of bowling pins, rolling and scattering into the ocean.

"We're sorry!" Nina called, hands cupped around her mouth. "We didn't mean to scare you. Please come back!"

As if they'd understood her words, the birds reemerged, lining up again along the beach and watching them alertly.

"This is a relief," Joel said. "I'm glad the penguins are okay."

Nina kneeled, holding her arms out. "Hi, everyone."

The birds turned skittish again, pressing into one another, the front row fully turning their backs on the Poppers. All except one, who made a loud *jook* and toddled forward. Once she had neared the family, she tilted her head to look at them inquiringly.

"What do you think she wants?" Nina asked.

"She wants us to feed her a fish, I'm sure of it!" Mrs. Popper said.

The penguin shook her head sharply, then raced into the surf, getting down onto her belly to slide like a toboggan until she'd disappeared underwater. She was gone under the surface for a minute, then emerged— with a fish in her mouth! She toddled up the beach until she was in front of Mrs. Popper, then dropped the wriggling fish onto the rock.

Mrs. Popper looked down at it.

"I think you're supposed to eat it," Joel whispered, nudging her.

"I am?" Mrs. Popper said through gritted teeth.

The penguin toddled forward, gave the wriggling fish a peck, and then looked up at Mrs. Popper expectantly. The penguin had a patch of extra white color on her head. That became her name in Joel's mind: Patch.

Mrs. Popper leaned down and managed to pick up the fish in her mittens. It stared at her with its big, bulging eyes, gills flaring.

She opened her mouth.

She closed her mouth.

Looking Patch in the eyes, to make sure she wasn't offending her, Mrs. Popper gave the fish a friendly pat.

Apparently that was enough of an acknowledgment

of the present. Patch gave a triumphant squawk and waddled back to the others. They greeted her in a joyful chorus, as if she'd just gotten back from a long journey.

"Negotiation successful!" Joel said.

Once the penguins' attention was drawn away, Mrs. Popper tossed the startled fish back into the ocean.

Nina looked disappointed. "We need that food!"

"Yes," Mrs. Popper said. "But I think we might want to cook our fish first."

"But you still didn't have to throw that one back!"

"Yes, I suppose that's true," Mrs. Popper said, smoothing the front of her coat. "I got flustered because I didn't know what to do, what can I say."

Right at that moment, another fish landed at the Poppers' feet. In fact, Joel realized, it might be the very same fish that Patch had brought them earlier. She'd emerged from the surf while they were talking and stood proudly over the retrieved fish.

"I think we'd better get a cooking fire started," Mrs. Popper said.

BLEAK PROSPECTS

THE POPPER PENGUINS would go right up to the doorway of the caretaker's hut, but they seemed unwilling to enter. They'd crowd in front of it, goading one another to go investigate, but none of them was willing to take the plunge and push open the door. Not even Patch was up to it, though she would occasionally work up the courage to spy through the window.

"Maybe they're worried that we're secretly sea lions

dressed up as humans and that we'll eat them right up," Joel said as he arranged his schoolbooks on the lumpy bed. His mother had informed him that, even in a survival situation, he'd have to keep up on his studies.

"It's silly for penguins to be afraid of us," Nina said. "At least Mae and Ernest aren't, are you?"

What Mae and Ernest were afraid of was the other penguins! The chicks hid behind the curtain covering the hut's window, occasionally peeking out at the big adult penguins, then hiding back away. Always the more

nervous of the two, Ernest had taken to diving under Mae for protection. Of course, only his head fit, so the rest of him splayed out on the windowsill.

"We aren't exactly raising the most courageous chicks the world has ever known, are we?" Mrs. Popper observed.

"It's only because they've led such sheltered lives so far," Nina said. "I think they'll find their place in the world once they've had time to adjust."

"I don't know, they seem to have a long way to go," Joel said. He sidled over to the hut's propane stove, its sole source of warmth. His mother was cooking a pair of fish on a pan. A third fish had been left raw and cut up on a tin plate, where it was serving as the chicks' meal. "When's our dinner ready?"

"In a few minutes," Mrs. Popper said. "Then I'll cook up a couple more fish to bring to Yuka."

"Well, we're definitely not going to run out of fish anytime soon," Nina said, pointing to the beach outside the window, where a neat pile of fish had accumulated. Whenever one of the penguins went on a fishing excursion, it would return with an extra fish to leave at the Poppers' door.

"I wonder if this is a trick Mr. Popper taught them years ago," Joel said.

"Our biggest danger won't be running out of food, but running out of fuel," Mrs. Popper said. "If that happens, we'll be very, very cold."

"How much is left?"

She rapped her knuckles against the side of the can. It rang out hollowly. "I'm not sure. I hope enough for a few days."

"You *hope*?" Nina said, her lower lip suddenly wobbling.

"Don't worry, darling," Mrs. Popper said. "The boat will be fixed by then. Or at least Yuka will have power restored so we can live on the boat until it's ready to make the return journey."

Joel kneeled down to stroke Mae's fuzzy back. "Maybe by then our chicks will be brave enough to introduce themselves to the other penguins."

"They're trying to find new parents," Nina said. "That can't be easy!"

"Yeah," Joel said, settling both chicks into his lap and petting them. "Don't let us rush you two."

Soon after Mrs. Popper was back from bringing

Yuka his cooked fish, nighttime dropped quick and dark. Still in their coats, the Popper family closed the hut's door, huddling together on the mattress with its scratchy but warm woolen blanket. The chicks tucked themselves under it.

The wind howled, each gust making the walls of the hut shudder. As he drifted toward sleep, Joel imagined a sea beast was hurling its tentacles against the hut. Popper Island was fun by day, but at night it was a strange and scary place. He was glad that they were all together, that he had Nina and his mother near. He hoped Yuka was okay.

Mae and Ernest burrowed closer as the wind got louder. Joel was glad that he had them alongside him, too.

The next morning, Nina was the first to wake. The air in the hut was so cold that it was hard to feel the tip of her nose. But under the wool blanket it was nice and warm. The wind had died down, and instead was... what *was* that sound?

Penguin chick snores! Nina held her ear against Ernest's beak and listened to the soft wheezy sound. Maybe he was dreaming—she could see his eyes moving rapidly beneath his lids.

Mrs. Popper sighed and got out of bed, opening the propane valve so she could light the stove. "You kids stay in bed until the hut's warmed up, okay?"

But Nina couldn't wait that long. She crept to the hut's door and eased it open.

The sunlight was bright over the thin layer of crackly ice that had formed on the pebbles of the beach. The Popper Penguins were already hard at work, toddling all over the shore, fishing and eating and carrying on. They would toss their heads back as they made loud calls to one another, exposing their beautiful long necks.

Joel joined Nina at the doorway, the chicks in his arms. He gently leaned down and released them onto the cold ground. They looked around, panicked, and then tried to retreat into the hut—until Nina closed the door behind them. They *oork*ed in protest.

"This is for your own good," Joel explained. "You have to get used to other penguins!"

The chicks looked out at the cold sea. It wasn't hard to imagine what they were thinking: Wouldn't it be so much nicer to stay in bed?

Patch tobogganed over and stood, toddling toward the frightened chicks. *"Jook!"* she said with a toss of her beak.

Ernest dived under Mae. Mae, though, looked bravely up at the strange penguin. Then she made her first adult penguin noise. *"Ork!"*

Patch clacked her beak against Mae's a few times. Clearly feeling emboldened, Ernest emerged and held his beak out, his eyes widening in delight when Patch clacked his, too.

Then the penguin walked along the beach, looking over her shoulder. The message was clear: *Come with me!*

That's just what Ernest and Mae did. After looking up at Nina and Joel for approval, they toddled after Patch.

"I think we'd better go along!" Joel said as the three penguins made their way along the beach.

"Mom, we're exploring with Mae and Ernest!" Nina called out. "We won't go far."

"Be very careful!" Mrs. Popper said. Another mother might not have let her children wander an Arctic island on their own. But Mrs. Popper knew that her kids would be careful.

"We'll be back by breakfast!" Joel called as he and his sister scrambled along the beach after their chicks and their new friend, rocks crunching under their feet.

"A penguin wants to show us something!" Nina huffed as she jogged along the beach, ice breaking and tinkling under her boots. "How exciting!"

SHOW AND TELL

AS THEY HIKED along the frozen beach, more and more of the Popper Penguins emerged from the surf to join them. Each time a new penguin neared, the chicks would go motionless, making their baby-like *oork* sounds, until they summoned enough courage to let out an adult *ork*. The process would repeat itself each time a new Popper Penguin joined the procession.

For such sleek creatures, the penguins were ungainly

on the shore. They tipped over this way and that the moment they hit a slippery patch, more often than not knocking over another bird in the process. Joel and Nina kept near the chicks, so they wouldn't inadvertently get squished by a rolling stranger.

Patch led them up a bank of rocks between the rough surfaces with her flexible feet. Many of the other penguins tried to make the jumps but gave up after a few dramatic falls. They made *ork*s of outrage as they retreated into the surf.

Mae courageously tried to make the first leap, but bonked her head on a protruding rock. She glared at it sternly. *"Gaw!"*

"Seems like you still need us," Nina said as she and Joel each picked up a chick and clambered up the rocks.

They drew their coats and scarves tighter as they crossed a windswept plateau. The ocean wind carried sprays of ice that stung their cheeks and noses. When they released the chicks to the ground, the birds seized up, holding their little wings tight to their bodies and scrunching their eyes closed. Joel and Nina each tucked a chick into their warm coats.

All the while, Patch led them along.

Popper Island wasn't large. Before twenty minutes had gone by, they were at the center. There, the penguin made a sharp turn, then brought them to the eastern edge.

Patch reached a precipice and turned around, making a loud *ork* as she gestured with one flipper.

Nina and Joel went to join her and saw that here the ground turned into a sharp cliff. Nesting down the vertical rocky surface were birds that looked a lot like penguins. They had the same white-and-black coloration, only they were smaller and had clown-like faces

that ended in bright red bills. Joel felt like they looked like inferior penguins. Then one spread its wings and swooped over the sea far below. They could fly. That was definitely a point in their favor.

"I think those are puffins!" Nina said. "Neat. I've always wanted to see a puffin."

The kids released Mae and Ernest so the chicks could see the puffins, too. It was clearly still too cold for them—they stuck to the warm nooks between the kids' legs. They did look out curiously, though, making startled little gasps whenever a puffin took flight. "I hope we're not making them jealous," Nina said, "not being able to fly and all."

Joel noticed that Patch kept pointing at the puffins with her wing. She wanted them to notice something.

He looked more closely. The puffins all seemed quite skinny. Some had tufts of hair sticking out in random places. They didn't look sleek like the island's penguins.

"I see eggshells around, but no chicks," Nina said. "That's odd, right?"

"And look!" Joel said. "The puffins will make short flights over the water, but they never return with any fish."

Mae and then Ernest toddled over to Patch, taking shelter beneath her belly. The penguin patiently accepted the chicks while she continued to point at the puffins. She made sad *ork*s, opening and closing her beak.

"I think I get it," Nina said, looking at the penguins and then the suffering puffin colony.

"What is it?" Joel asked.

"The puffins were the only birds around before. So they were the only ones eating the local fish. But now there are all these penguins here."

"...and the penguins are eating all the good fish," Joel said, "which means there's not enough food left for the puffins."

Patch made a satisfied-sounding *ork*. These dense humans had finally figured out what was going on.

A GATHERING STORM

WHEN THE CHILDREN returned to the caretaker's hut, they found Yuka and their mother standing outside. They looked like adults often do when they're worried—very still, arms crossed, staring hard. Joel and Nina sped up, in case they were the reason the grown-ups were anxious. But their mother kept her arms crossed even after she'd seen them.

"Oh, good, you're back," she said.

"What's going on?" Joel asked, shading his eyes against the low sun, trying to see what had captured all of his mother's attention.

Yuka shook his head and put on a tight smile. "Nothing you need to concern yourselves about."

"There's no point hiding it from them," Mrs. Popper said. "Kids deserve to know the truth."

"*What* truth?" Nina asked, her face turning red.

"The boat is nearly fixed," Yuka said, his face lighting up.

"Oh," Joel said, confused. "That's *good* news, right?"

"Yes," he said. "I just wanted to start with some of that. Ahem. The bad news is that, well, you can see for yourself." Yuka pointed to the southern sky, where a bank of dark clouds had formed.

"That *does* look like bad news," Nina said, nodding.

"It's coming our way," Mrs. Popper explained, "and an arctic storm is serious business. We can't sail out until it's passed over."

"And we don't know when it will end," Yuka said. "If my instruments had been working correctly, we'd have known about it on our way here and could have headed to the mainland earlier."

A mournful *oork* came from within Joel's coat. "I think Ernest is very sorry about the sabotage," Joel said.

"Yuka will be staying with us in the hut while the storm is raging," Mrs. Popper said.

"We've got a few hours left," he said. "Your mother wants to stay here to get the hut ready, but would you two come with me to the boat? We need to retrieve whatever supplies we can before the wind and snow come. There will be no crossing the island later."

Nina and Joel nodded somberly. "Of course."

Together they hiked across the island to the boat and returned with as many supplies as they could carry— which was not, truth be told, all that many. A lot of them had been lost overboard during the wreck.

When they returned to the caretaker's hut, Yuka and Joel and Nina each had a crate in their arms. They piled them in a corner of the room. Ernest and Mae hopped down from the windowsill, where they had been keeping tabs on the Popper Penguins. They huddled into the comfort of the kids' ankles.

The wind outside began to howl. Yuka looked out the window at the sky, his expression turning grim. "Maybe there's less time than I thought. There might be long enough for only one more trip to the boat."

"I'm ready," Nina said.

"No, you two stay here," Yuka said. "I don't want to risk your being trapped outside when the winds start."

They watched from the window as Yuka headed back to his boat. Once he'd disappeared from view, Mrs. Popper clapped her hands briskly. "Let's get everything put away, so the hut's in the best order we can get it. We might be stuck inside for a long time."

Ernest and Mae watched gravely as the Poppers

prepared the hut. Joel shook out the spare coverlet and draped it over a makeshift bed of pillows on the floor, so Yuka would have somewhere to sleep. Nina and Mrs. Popper lined up the food supplies. "Lots of canned beans!" Nina announced.

"And some tuna fish, I hope?" Joel asked, patting Ernest on the head.

"Of course," Nina said. "Though I think *we're* going to eat that, now that the penguins have been delivering raw fish."

"Oh no, the Popper Penguins!" Joel said, peering out the hut's small window. "Do you think they're going to be okay, Mom?"

She squeezed Joel's shoulder. "Of course they'll be okay. They've survived many winters out here. They're designed for this sort of weather. It's primates like us who have to worry."

When Yuka reappeared at the doorway, he had icicles hanging from his hood, and the stubble on his chin glittered with frost. The wind roared into the hut, scattering the pillows Joel had carefully arranged and knocking over a tower of canned beans. Yuka slammed the door closed and stamped his booted feet. "Wow. I guess I went through storms like this in my childhood, but this seems worse than any of those ever were."

"Were you able to radio the authorities while you were at the boat?" Mrs. Popper asked.

Yuka shook his head. "No, sorry. The electrical systems aren't up yet. But we're going to be fine. And the Popper Foundation knows our itinerary, so if we're missing for long enough, they'll be sure to send help."

The walls shuddered. Ernest made an *oork* of panic and hopped onto the bed.

"I think Ernest has the right idea," Joel said, zipping his coat up tight before following the penguin chick under the covers.

STRANGE BEDFELLOWS

THE NEXT TWO days passed in a blur. Once the storm clouds covered the arctic sun, there was little outside light coming into the hut, so it was hard to know whether it was day or night. It didn't much matter, anyway—there was no going outside, whatever time it was. All Nina knew was that the tempest shook the roof and set the walls trembling, that it snaked cold fingers under the door and through the double-paned glass of the window, that the only defense was to huddle under the comforter, hoping the storm didn't decide to take the roof off entirely.

By drawing her hood strings tight, Nina was able to have only her nose exposed. But even so, she could feel her body growing colder. Though she knew it would make her arm tingle from the cold air, she reached out to touch the heater. It felt like ice.

Nina tucked her arm back under the covers. "Mom," she said softly, "I think the propane ran out."

"Oh no," Mrs. Popper said. She reached out, touched the stove, and gasped. "You're right. Huddle down, children. Are you okay, Yuka?"

"Yes," he said from his pile of pillows. But he couldn't keep the shivers out of his voice.

The winds continued to howl, and the temperature continued to drop. Joel and Nina drew close to their mother, snuggling in as near as they could—even though under any other circumstances, Joel would have claimed he was too old for such a thing.

"Don't worry, kids," Mrs. Popper said. Nina knew her mother only said that when she *was* worried, of course.

"I'm not afraid!" Nina said.

"Me neither!" Joel said. Nina could almost believe him.

Despite their worry, they all grew sleepy, and gradually Nina sensed her thoughts growing scattered. Then she must have fallen asleep, because she became aware of waking up. The wind was howling louder than ever, and as she fully opened her eyes, she realized why.

Someone had opened the door.

"Mom!" Nina said urgently. But her mother kept snoring.

Long shadows grew across the floor as the intruder—no, intruders—came in closer.

Their shadows were shaped sort of like bowling pins.

It was the Popper Penguins. At least two dozen Popper Penguins.

The birds were lined up in the doorway, facing in. Mae and Ernest must have sensed their kind nearby. They rolled onto the ground from under the comforter and were facing the adult penguins, making nervous *oork* sounds.

Nina nudged her brother. "Joel. *Penguins!* In the hut!"

He grunted and rolled over in his sleep, pulling the wool blanket over his head.

The Popper Penguins waddled forward, cautiously investigating the hut, taking careful pecks of the cabinets, the walls, the boots lined up by the doorway. Once the first ones had freed up space in the opening, more filed in from behind. Nina wouldn't have thought penguins ever could look cold, but these ones certainly did. They had frost on their feathered eyebrows, along their beaks, on the tips of their dark, dinosaur-like feet.

Nina nudged Joel again. "*More* penguins!"

Soon they'd filled the entire floor of the hut, their *ork*s and *jook*s filling the air, while the wind from the storm outside whistled.

Once the last of the Popper Penguins was inside the shelter of the hut, Patch pressed her flipper against the door and pushed it closed.

Even though Joel had managed to sleep through the clamor of a roomful of penguins, *that* sound was what woke him up. "Wow" was all he could think to say.

Yuka sat up amid his pillows. "I guess they must be cold, too."

Surprised by Yuka's deep voice, the penguins panicked, tumbling over one another, bumping into the walls and cabinets before heaping into a great squawking pile. Once the two dozen penguins had righted themselves, Yuka was trapped, sitting bolt upright in the center of them. His eyebrows disappeared right into his hairline, he was that surprised.

"Kids," he said, "I'm stuck in a waddle of penguins!"

"Do you need help?" Nina asked, tugging on her furry slippers.

Yuka considered the question for a moment. "No, actually," he said, appearing to surprise even himself. "This is may be the coziest I've been in my whole life. Turns out penguins are excellent insulators!"

Before anyone could stop her, Nina had scrambled

out of bed and into the midst of the birds. They made their panicked noises again but didn't bowl one another over this time. They were more comfortable with Nina.

"Oh, wow," Nina said. "He's right. This is amazing!"

Joel joined her in the huddle of penguins. Their feathery coats were smooth and warm and smelled of fish and seawater. "Whoa. It's really nice."

Just then their mother woke up. "Kids, where are you?" she asked as she cleared the sleep from her eyes. Her jaw dropped wide open once she saw her children and Yuka, waving at her from the huddle of penguins.

"You have to try this, Mom!" Nina said.

THE HUDDLE

CROWDING IN WITH penguins turned out to be a wonderful way to ride out a storm. The birds were amazingly warm and soft. But it was more than that. Even though fearsome things were happening, even after the propane ran out and arctic night fell and the wind howled louder and louder, the penguins kept up a stream of chatter. It was a great distraction—it was harder to stay scared when there was so much to eavesdrop on.

"I think this tall one next to me doesn't like the short

one next to you," Nina said to Joel. "He keeps throwing his head back and making a lot of noise in the short one's direction."

"I think that's because he *does* like him," Joel said. "This short one is the warmest of them all."

"What are you kids talking about?" Mrs. Popper called out. She was pinned between penguins, just like the rest of them, only she was stuck on the far side of the hut.

"The puffins are starving!" Nina said, but her voice was lost in the ruckus of penguin cries.

"What did you say?" Mrs. Popper shouted.

"We'll tell you later!" Nina said.

"WHAT?"

"WE'LL TELL YOU—never mind," Nina said, letting her voice get lost in the bird chorus.

Come dawn, the winds died down and the penguins filed out of the hut one by one, each taking a moment to wave goodbye before heading off to fish. "I'm getting the sense that this isn't the first time the penguins have ridden out the worst of a storm by keeping warm in the hut," Joel said, stretching his arms and legs to get the blood circulating again.

"I'm sure they're able to tolerate the most extreme

cold, but I can't blame them for taking a better option when it becomes available! No wonder the caretaker needed a break," Mrs. Popper said. "I'm not sure how much more I could take of that."

"I thought it was fantastic," Nina said. "And they have good skills with door handles!"

"Yeah, I kind of miss them already," Joel added. He swooped down to pick up Ernest and Mae, who were looking around with astonished expressions on their faces, as if debating whether the flood of adult penguins had been a dream.

He was answered by a *plop, plop, plop* from the open doorway. Joel peered out. During the storm the rocks of Popper Island had disappeared under a layer of white snow and ice, sparkling in the morning sun. On top of that ice lay three fish.

Before Joel's eyes, Patch emerged from the surf, waddled over, and regurgitated a fish onto the ice. It was a terrific production, with lots of hacking and heaving and shrieking. The fish was slick with stomach fluids.

"Ew," Joel said, even as Ernest and Mae hopped down from his arms, toddled over, and scarfed down the fish with *ork*s of joy.

"That's good," Nina said, pulling her hat low over her ears as she joined Joel in the doorway. "I'm glad Ernest and Mae took care of that, because I don't think I was up for eating barf fish."

"Yes," Joel replied. "I'm with you."

Yuka slipped out of the hut and walked right past the penguin-puked fish, unimpressed. The spiky crampons on his boots crunched through the fresh ice as he headed to the boat. "Back to work! I'm hoping to be finished with the repair by the end of the day."

"Thank you, Yuka!" Mrs. Popper called from within the hut.

Joel looked at Ernest, who had just finished gobbling down his second fish. Ernest looked up at Joel proudly, fluttering his fuzzy wings.

"Ernest and Mae haven't made any penguin friends yet," Nina said.

"I'm worried about them, too," Joel said. "There's only a few hours left, and we don't know if they'll be okay after we leave."

A NEW DESTINATION

JOEL AND NINA and Mrs. Popper lined up on the shoreline, looking at the rocking boat. Beaten metal covered the hole the Popper Island shoals had made in the hull. Yuka had neatly welded it on with strips of light gray solder. "Looks pretty good, right?" Yuka said, rapping his knuckles on the hull. It rang out brightly.

"It does. Great work!" Mrs. Popper said.

Joel tried to add his voice, but the pit in his stomach

was making it hard even to speak. Ernest was tight in his arms, snoring away.

How was Joel going to say what he needed to say?

Nina looked up at him. Normally she was the more assertive one, but apparently it was his turn this time around.

"Are you two okay?" Mrs. Popper asked.

"Yeah," Joel said, nodding. Then he shook his head. "No. I mean, no."

"Yes, right, no," Nina said, nodding her head energetically and then shaking it just as energetically.

"You're both acting very peculiar."

"No kidding," Yuka said, narrowing his eyes. "I know none of us slept too well the last few nights, but you're being really weird."

"Okay, here goes," Joel said, taking his mom's hand and looking into her eyes so she would know to listen hard to him. "One of the penguins took us to the other side of the island, and there are puffins there, which should be great, but they're not healthy, not at all, they're all scrawny and their eggs are broken but there aren't any chicks, and the penguins are all fat and healthy, and we think that the problem is the penguins are eating all the fish around here and there's none left for the puffins, and they were here *first*, so that doesn't seem fair, does it?"

Mrs. Popper stared at him, her mouth wide open. Then she finally put together his stream of words. She nodded. "So what do you want us to do?"

Nina coughed and stepped forward, maybe a little dramatically. "It might have been a good idea in the olden days for Mr. Popper to bring his penguins up here, but he didn't realize that it would make it hard for the puffins to survive, even all these generations later. What if... what if we brought them to where they belong?"

"You mean, to the *Ant*arctic?" Mrs. Popper said, hand over her chest.

"That's, um, very far from here," Yuka added.

"Yes," Nina said, tears entering her voice. "But then the penguins would all be in their proper home, with other penguins. And during the voyage Mae and Ernest would have more of a chance to bond with the rest of the group and find penguins to be their parents."

Mrs. Popper looked at Yuka. His face was completely still. Then, finally, he gave a little shrug. "If you all help me pilot, I could write my paper and send it to my professor along the way."

"And we have the winter break not so far off," Nina said quickly. "We'd only miss a couple extra weeks of school. In the meantime, we can work ahead in our textbooks."

"It would be *so* educational for us to go to Antarctica, don't you think?" Joel said.

"Yes, Mom, it's an opportunity not to be missed," Nina said, nodding eagerly.

Mrs. Popper looked at her children, then at the dozing Mae and Ernest, tight in their arms. "I suppose we could see if it's possible."

Nina jumped up and down, then remembered Mae and stopped. The penguin chick didn't wake, though—she must not have slept in the ruckus last night, either. She gave a soft, fish-scented burp while she slept.

"But, kids," Mrs. Popper said, "just how do you propose we get two dozen wild penguins to board a boat?"

Joel paused. They'd been so busy worrying about how to convince Mom that they hadn't considered *this* problem.

Yuka coughed. "The ancestors of these penguins arrived here on a boat, so maybe it won't be so very unfamiliar to them."

"You mean the penguins might have been passing down stories about their trip here?" Mrs. Popper asked, eyebrows raised.

"Stranger things have happened," Yuka said, shrugging.

Nina tugged on her mom's sleeve. "Mom, *Mom*! If that's true, maybe they've been passing down other stories about the original Popper Penguins. Remember, they used to have a *circus act*, where they *marched in formation*?"

Joel realized where his sister was going, and clapped. That woke Ernest up, who gave an outraged grunt and rolled over to fall back asleep in Joel's arms.

THE POPPER PENGUINS
PERFORM AN ENCORE

BACK IN THE 1930s, Popper's Performing Penguins had paraded onstage to the "Merry Widow Waltz" on the piano. That was all well and good if you were getting penguins to march in a music hall, but there were no pianos on Popper Island.

The modern-day Poppers made do, though, by standing outside the caretaker's hut and banging on camping pots with spoons. They tried to be as rhythmic and musical as possible, but Joel and Nina kept losing each other's beats, so it was really more of a ruckus than a song. Still, the penguins lined up curiously on the beach, watching the noisemakers and adding *gorks* and *gaws* of their own, making shy turns and pirouettes.

When the Poppers began to make their way across the icy rocks from the beach to the boat, Nina almost didn't dare look back to see if the penguins were behind them. But when she did, there was the line of penguins,

following single file, adding their chorus of voices to the glorious noise.

"The Arctic will never see anything like this again," Yuka said. From the look on his face, he thought that was for the best.

When they reached the boat, the Poppers went right to the bow to make as much space as possible. There they all were: Mrs. Popper and Nina and Joel, still banging on camping pots, Mae and Ernest at their feet. The rest of the deck was wall-to-wall penguins, with Yuka at the stern, gently nudging away the nearby birds so he could start the boat's engine.

When the deck began to rumble under their feet, the penguins *ork*ed and milled about, bumping into one another and pecking curiously at the floor. Mae and Ernest imitated the big penguins, even though by now they knew perfectly well how the boat worked.

After taking up the anchor, Yuka steered away from Popper Island.

Joel and Nina stood at the stern, surrounded by their new penguin friends as they looked back at Popper Island. Two puffins were standing at their cliff, watching the departing boat. In unison, they each raised a wing.

"It's like they're saying goodbye," Joel said.

"Or maybe they're saying thank you," Nina said.

"Good luck, puffins!" Joel called, waving.

"Okay, children. Get working on your homework while there's still light out and the waves aren't too rough, please," Mrs. Popper called. "As soon as we're near enough to shore I'll call and get your updated assignments."

"You'd think that when we're sailing through the Arctic with two dozen penguins, we could skip the normal school rules," Nina grumbled.

"Not when it's our mom," Joel said.

With that, they were off! The penguins were fascinated by all aspects of the trip: the whitewater at the stern, the rumbling engines, the seabirds wheeling overhead. Much to Yuka's dismay, they were especially interested in the steering wheel, taking pecks at it as soon as his attention was distracted. Joel had to shoo Ernest away whenever he got renewed interest in investigating the boat's repaired computer.

Before Popper Island disappeared from view, they saw a puffin one more time, soaring over the water, swooping to catch a fish before heading back home.

GROWING PAINS

IT TOOK THEM six weeks to reach the Antarctic. By
that point Nina and Joel had gotten ahead on all their
schoolwork and were learning side topics: avian biology
for Joel and lines of latitude for Nina. They'd stopped
in Hillport to stock up on fish, to get permission to tem-
porarily withdraw the kids from school, and for Yuka
to turn in his essay and pick up his research books so he
could work on his dissertation during the voyage.

The Popper Foundation understood when the Poppers explained that the penguins had been outcompeting the native puffins in the Arctic. They gave Mrs. Popper and Yuka stipends to compensate them for their work in relocating the penguins, and also paid for a refrigeration unit to be installed belowdecks—the penguins would need to stay down there while the boat passed through the hot tropics. (Two sneaked out onto the deck anyway one night, and the kids found them there in the morning, overheating, flippers flung out wide and mouths open. They never tried to sneak out again after that!)

By the time the boat had rounded the bottom of Argentina and was nearing the Antarctic, Mae and Ernest started to look...odd. "I think Mae is sick!" Nina said. She held up the penguin's wing so Joel could see her torso beneath, where a patch of gray fluffy feathers was missing.

"She's not sick," Joel said, pointing to a picture in the avian biology textbook they'd checked out from the Hillport library. "She's molting. The same thing is happening to Ernest."

"It's normal?" Nina asked.

"Totally normal."

Over the final days of the voyage, Mae and Ernest would do their usual preening, nipping at their feathers, only now big clumps of them would come away. Beneath were revealed sleek black feathers—their adult plumage! "Would you look at that," Nina said. "Our little penguins are growing up!"

"They look kind of like punk rockers," Joel said.

They might have started getting their adult feathers, but even over the six weeks of voyage, the chicks had yet to bond with the other penguins. While Joel was busy with his homework, Ernest would stand near the other

birds, but the whole time he'd be looking over at Joel, as if asking whether he was allowed to come back yet. Mae was clearer about her feelings: She'd pick fights if any Popper Penguins came between her and Nina, only calming once she was back in her arms.

"They'll start fitting in eventually, right?" Nina asked Mrs. Popper.

"I'm sure," her mother replied. "Soon we'll be at the Drake Research Station, and we can ask the penguin experts there how we can help Mae and Ernest adjust. Now, it's getting chillier. Draw your scarves tight, children."

The very next day, Yuka called out and slowed the boat. The penguins all gathered at the bow to see what had gotten his attention. Shore!

A glacier ran right up against the water, its surfaces going from white at the edges to a brilliant blue in its core. At the far end of the giant block of ice was a gravelly beach that rose up to a stony bluff. On top was a simple red building, with aluminum sides and a peaked, snow-covered roof.

"That's the Drake Center for Environmental Studies," Yuka said. "I've read a lot about it in my courses. They're doing important research about our climate.

Who would have thought life would come to this—I grew up near the North Pole, but now I'm at the very other end of the planet!"

As they watched, a figure emerged from the little red building and stood at the edge of the cliff. She waved at them as she brought a megaphone to her mouth. "Hello! I'm Dr. Antonia Drake. Welcome! You can bring your boat right up to the slip."

"Oh, good," Yuka said under his breath. "No ship-wrecks this time."

By the time he had guided the boat to the dock, and Joel and Nina had hopped to shore to tie it up tight, Dr. Drake had come down to greet them. "What a long journey you've had," she said. "You must be so tired."

"Not really!" Nina said. "We're mostly just excited."

"Who's that?" Dr. Drake asked, looking at the small penguin by Nina's feet.

"That's Mae," Joel explained. "And this is Ernest. They look like adults now, but they just finished molting. They're the reason we started on this whole adventure!"

In fact, Ernest hadn't quite finished molting. He still had a tuft of fluffy feathers on the back of his head, like an old balding man.

"They need a little help learning to socialize—" Mrs. Popper said, then she had to stop and concentrate on not falling into the sea as twenty-four penguins marched along the boat and hopped past her onto the dock, nearly knocking her over in the process.

Patch walked to the water's edge, stared in, then walked back. She mustered enough courage to return to the edge, then lost her nerve again and waddled back. Patch walked to the edge again, but this time another penguin crowded in behind her to see and accidentally knocked her in! She made a *gork* as she bobbed on the surface, then dived away. Since no seals had eaten the first penguin yet, the others plopped in after her.

"They seem to be making themselves right at home, don't they?" Dr. Drake said, laughing.

"All except our two little leftovers from the Penguin Pavilion," Nina said.

Only Ernest and Mae remained on land.

They looked up at the Popper children.

They looked down at the cold sea.

Ernest headed into the galley and started making his little-chick *oork* sounds as he perused the cans of fish.

"I see what you mean," Dr. Drake said, tapping her

gloved finger against her lips as she considered the two odd young penguins. "They don't seem to have made any progress getting used to being with other penguins. None at all."

Mae waddled over to the ship's radio and pecked the power button. She lay back and listened to the music, bouncing her flippers in rhythm with the beats.

HOMECOMING

ONCE THEY HAD finished filling their bellies with fish—"And squid," Dr. Drake said, "that's really their primary diet around here"—the penguins filed onto land. The Poppers and Dr. Drake lined up at the shore to watch. "This is a novel environment for the Popper Penguins," Dr. Drake explained while Joel took notes. "They're bound to be apprehensive about what they'll find. We should expect them to be insecure and to stick near the boat for a long time."

As they emerged from the surf, though, the Popper Penguins walked in the opposite direction, heading right into the wilds of Antarctica. "Oh!" said Dr. Drake.

Once the adult birds had marched past, Mae and Ernest made their sleepy sounds and toddled toward their nests in the boat. "Nope," Nina said. "You're not going to bed now—we just got here!"

She and Joel scooped up the young birds and headed after the line of penguins. Mrs. Popper and Dr. Drake and Yuka hustled to keep up. "This is most unexpected," Dr. Drake said. "These particular birds have never been to Antarctica, though their forebears of course came from here. Nonetheless, they're taking their ancestral routes over the ice. It's as if no time has gone by!"

"Penguins are very smart," Nina said, nodding. "You should have seen Mae at school. Can't say she was much help on my spelling test, though."

"The Popper Penguins seem to be an especially intelligent line," Mrs. Popper added. "They were able to learn sophisticated dance moves, and their act toured theaters across the country."

"Is it possible that the Popper Penguins have somehow passed along knowledge of where they came from, over all these years?" Yuka asked, rummaging through his backpack with his gloved hands to get his research notebook out.

Dr. Drake shook her head. "Preposterous. That would require them to have language. Not just simple communication, but the ability to capture verb tenses, to refer to places by name. Even the most advanced chimpanzees can't do that."

"I think there are a lot of things we might not know about penguins," Nina said, patting Mae on the head. "I'm positive that she and Ernest have really in-depth conversations with each other."

"Mostly about where their next can of tuna fish is coming from," Joel added.

"I know that to a child's eyes it can seem like animals have magical powers of communication, but the science doesn't back that up," Dr. Drake said as they marched.

Nina had been working her way ahead of the group. She whirled around, arms outstretched. "Then what do you say to *that*?" she asked.

They'd reached a rise in the icy field that looked out

over a broad blue-white valley. It was covered in hundreds and hundreds of penguins, waddling to and fro. They clustered in the center of the basin, where the dense crowd *ork*ed and *jook*ed and *gaw*ed, courted and canoodled and fought. Some of the penguins were sitting on nests they'd cobbled together with small rocks, and before Nina's eyes one toddled over to the nest next door, stole a rock, and waddled it back to his own nest. Then the original owner of the rock noticed the theft and waddled over to steal the rock right back, starting a penguin fight that soon involved a half dozen neighbors.

Similar episodes were going on throughout the massive penguin colony. There was so much to see, like in a picture book where each time you looked there was some new tiny story to discover in the illustrations.

"This is the biggest gentoo colony in Antarctica," Dr. Drake said proudly. "We've had a continuous study site here for over a hundred years."

"Gentoo?" Joel asked. "What's that?"

"There are many species of penguins in the world. Gentoo is the name of the species of the Popper Penguins. My grandfather sent Mr. Popper his original penguin from this very colony."

"Oh," Joel said.

"Oh my!" Mrs. Popper interrupted. "Have you seen what's going on over there?"

"That's what I was talking about before!" Nina protested. "*Now* do you believe me?"

"Wow," Yuka said.

"Well, I never," Mrs. Popper said.

The Popper Penguins, fresh off their trip from the Arctic, had waddled and tobogganed right into the middle of the gentoo colony. There they'd lined up in a row, making quiet *ork*s that sounded almost like coughs, waiting for the attention of the other birds. And attention is just what they got. A ruckus rose from the colony as they noticed the strangers. Those that weren't tending nests came right over, crowding in, knocking one another over to get the best view, making a deafening chorus of penguin calls.

Once they had the attention of the other penguins, the Popper Penguins began to perform.

While the Antarctic penguins watched, Patch lay on the ice for a long pause, then pretended to wake up and stand and look about. Another penguin joined her, peering about dramatically. They were followed by ten more, until there were twelve penguins in all. They marched in a perfect circle, all waddling in unison, then formed a square before becoming a semicircle. Two of them separated from the group and got into a mock fight, buffeting each other with their flippers and biting the air. They both fell over, as if dead.

"They're performing Nelson and Columbus!" Nina exclaimed.

"Oh no, does that mean the ladder-and-board act from the original show is next?" Joel asked, covering his eyes. "I heard that was a complete disaster."

As they watched, the twelve penguins marched in formation up an ice cliff, where they crowded at the summit. Then they went completely still.

"What's supposed to happen now?" Mrs. Popper asked.

"I'm not sure," Joel said.

The audience of a thousand penguins and five humans began to murmur.

Then Patch let out an ear-piercing cry. As one, the penguins made a great show of pushing one another to the ground, tobogganing off the peak in all directions, letting out loud squawks as they tumbled away before getting to their feet again down at the bottom, appearing very proud of themselves. It all looked a bit like a firework display, only made of penguins.

Once they were finished, the Popper Penguins lined themselves back up in a straight line, while the Antarctic penguins broke out into a raucous chorus of *ork*s and *gaw*s. The Popper Penguins took neat bows, or at least as best they were able with their stout bodies. (It was difficult to bow without a waist.)

The gentoos surged forward, crowding around the Popper Penguins, greeting them with a frantic display of clacking beaks and loud calls. They lifted the Popper Penguins so they surfed over the top of the colony, making *ork*s of delight as they accepted the crowd's admiration.

"Well, I'll be!" Yuka said.

"The scientific world has never seen anything like this," Dr. Drake marveled.

"The Popper Penguins passed down stories about Antarctica *and* Stillwater!" Nina said.

"Maybe they'll keep passing these stories down in the wild colony here," Yuka proposed.

"Fascinating," said Dr. Drake. "We'll need to publish studies on this right away. Are you prepared to work with me, Yuka?"

"I'm revising my dissertation in my head right now!" he said. He and Dr. Drake then descended into a lot of scientific language that Nina and Joel couldn't understand at all.

Their attention was soon drawn to the young chicks at their feet. Mae and Ernest had enjoyed the Popper show, jumping up and down in glee and doing their own pantomime version of the specialized steps along with the Popper Penguins. But now they looked almost mournful. Head down, Ernest was already making his slow waddling progress back to the boat. Mae made an *oork* that sounded very familiar to the Popper kids by now: She was ready for some canned tuna fish. Ernest made an *oork* that they also knew very well: It was time for his favorite nature program on the ship's shortwave radio.

Joel gave Nina a long look. Their plan for getting the two young chicks back to the wild wasn't working out. Not at all.

FAREWELL, DR. DRAKE

WHILE JOEL AND Nina holed up in the research station, they heard a clamor from the icy valley as the Popper Penguins gave yet another command performance.

The Popper children weren't out enjoying the show, though—they were too worried about Mae and Ernest. The young penguins were eating dried squid from a pile on the floor, in between moves in their version of chess. Joel and Nina hadn't been able to figure out the rules yet, but it seemed to involve a lot of pecking and fighting and pawns flying everywhere.

"It's almost like they don't know that they're penguins," Joel said.

"I'd say that's exactly right," Dr. Drake said from the doorway. Nina and Joel looked up, startled. "When they're born, young birds go through a process called imprinting. In order to learn the right habits and bird manners, they study whatever animal they first see when they hatch. Normally that's another penguin, of course. In this case, though, it was you!"

"But the original Popper Penguins were able to go live in the wild," Nina protested.

Dr. Drake nodded. "You'll remember that Mr. Popper's first penguin, Captain Cook, was an adult. When *he* was a chick, he'd been around other penguins. By the time chicks were in Stillwater, they had other penguins around to imprint on. These two weren't in the same situation, unfortunately. It's not your fault—you did the best you could with these eggs. But I'm afraid they won't survive out here in the wild without parents, just like human children wouldn't."

With that, Mae let out a loud squid burp as she picked

up a black rook with her beak, deftly depositing it on the other side of the board. Ernest squawked in outrage at the move, then settled down. He gently tapped each of the white pieces with his beak, considering his options.

"It's true, there aren't many chess sets in the wild," Joel said.

"Or nature hours for Ernest to listen to on the radio," Nina added.

"I suspect these aren't gentoos, either, but Magellanic penguins. Those penguins don't even live in the Antarctic, but in South America. To be honest, Ernest might be female and Mae might be male. I could be wrong on that, though—even after all these years working with penguins, it's still hard for me to tell the sexes apart without a blood test."

"Oh my," Nina said.

Just then there was a clamor outside as the Popper Penguins finished their big act. Mrs. Popper and Yuka burst in, breathless. "This was the best show yet!" Mrs. Popper said. "The Popper Penguins have really gotten their comic timing down. I'm proud of them."

"At least the Popper Penguins have found a good home," Joel said. "They're basically celebrities down here."

Nina threw her arms around her mother's waist, burying her face in the pockets of her puffy coat. "Mae and Ernest aren't even the same *species* as all these other penguins, Mom," she cried.

"Oh dear," Mrs. Popper said. "What would you suggest, Dr. Drake? What's best for our little penguins?"

"They can't live in the wild, but they could do a lot of good for the penguins that *do*," Dr. Drake said. "As the planet warms from human activity, this ice is melting, and the penguins' homeland is in greater and greater danger. Sometimes we lose entire colonies of penguins because of the melting ice down here. It sounds like the Penguin Pavilion didn't do things right, but *you* could. What if you brought Mae and Ernest to visit schools in the winter, when it's cold enough for them to be out and about, so kids everywhere could learn about penguins? Other times of year, scientists and interested children could come visit your birds in your frozen basement. I'm sure the Popper Foundation would be interested in funding such a place, with you as the caretaker."

Mrs. Popper looked surprised. "Money has been tight, and I'd be honored to do something to help the penguins. I've been making some charcoal sketches of the Popper show. Maybe I could sell art of Mae and Ernest, to support the Popper Foundation's work."

Nina kept her arms around her mother but pulled her head back to look up, amazed. "Really?" she said, her face streaked with tears.

Joel jumped up and down. "This is amazing! We're going to keep Mae and Ernest!"

The penguins in question scolded the humans for their interruption, before returning to their chess game.

"I'm going to stay down here with Dr. Drake, writing my dissertation on the transmission of knowledge between generations of gentoo penguins," Yuka said. "But I'll need to go back up to Stillwater first to draft my study plan with my professor. I could take you—and our two young penguin ambassadors—up with me."

"That's great news, Yuka," Mrs. Popper said. "And great news for the gentoo penguins, that they'll be the subjects of your study."

"It's just about as far away from home as an Inuit can get," he said. "My family will miss me for a few years."

"I'm sure they'll be very proud of your contribution to science," Mrs. Popper said.

"I hope so!"

And so it was that only a few days later, the Popper family and their two young penguins lined up at the stern of the boat. "Just think, Joel!" Nina said. "We're going to be bringing our penguins back to school, after all!"

"And for a good purpose this time," Joel added.

The boat began to pull away from the dock. In unison, Mae and Ernest made a new kind of noise, a sort of *yewk*.

"What does that call mean?" Mrs. Popper asked as she waved goodbye to Dr. Drake.

"I think it means they're content," Joel said.

" 'Content,' " Nina said. "That word was on my spelling test, once upon a time."

"Content is a very nice thing for a young penguin to be," Mrs. Popper said.

Yuka blasted the boat's horn, and with that sound the Poppers waved goodbye to Antarctica. Joel and Nina lifted the penguins so that they could say goodbye, too, which they did dramatically, waving their flippers as hard as they could. Then Yuka sped the boat up, and they were plowing through the waves, heading back home and to whatever adventures it held in store.

ACKNOWLEDGMENTS

I'm so grateful to Florence and Richard Atwater for crafting one of the true classics of children's literature, full of fun and adventure—and a great respect for animals. The Atwaters created a world in which truly magical events occurred (like a penguin being mailed from the Antarctic!) yet also treated the Poppers' experience living with penguins realistically and believably. *Mr. Popper's Penguins* is full of heart and whimsy, and it was a delight to get to pay homage to their vision. I once stayed up late on a school night to finish *Mr. Popper's Penguins*—I wish I could go back and tell that young Eliot what was to come three decades later!

Nikki Garcia, my editor at Little, Brown Books for Young Readers—thanks to you and Alvina Ling for working so hard to get this book across the finish line and into readers' hands. You and the copy editors and the marketing and publicity team have been marvels.

Thanks as well to people who read manuscripts:

Richard Pine (my stalwart literary agent), kid reader James Driskill, and my circle of writer friends: Daphne Benedis-Grab, Jill Santopolo, Marie Rutkoski, Marianna Baer, Anne Heltzel, and Anna Godbersen. Special thanks to Eric Zahler and Barbara Schrefer.

Extra thanks are due as well to the Atwater estate, Kate and Alec Bishop, for trusting me with this continuation of the Popper Penguin story. Your feedback and insights have been invaluable.

Ork!

Turn the page for a preview of

A NEWBERY HONOR BOOK

Mr. Popper's PENGUINS

FLORENCE AND RICHARD ATWATER

AVAILABLE NOW

STILLWATER

IT WAS AN afternoon in late September. In the pleasant little city of Stillwater, Mr. Popper, the house painter, was going home from work.

He was carrying his buckets, his ladders, and his boards so that he had rather a hard time moving along. He was spattered here and there with paint and calcimine, and there were bits of wallpaper clinging to his hair and whiskers, for he was rather an untidy man.

The children looked up from their play to smile at him as he passed, and the housewives, seeing him, said, "Oh dear, there goes Mr. Popper. I must remember to ask John to have the house painted over in the spring."

No one knew what went on inside of Mr. Popper's head, and no one guessed that he would one day be the most famous person in Stillwater.

He was a dreamer. Even when he was busiest smoothing down the paste on the wallpaper, or painting the outside of other people's houses, he would forget what he was doing. Once he had painted three sides of a kitchen green, and the other side yellow. The housewife, instead of being angry and making him do it over, had liked it so well that she had made him leave it that way. And all the other housewives, when they saw it, admired it too, so that pretty soon everybody in Stillwater had two-colored kitchens.

The reason Mr. Popper was so absent-minded was that he was always dreaming about far-away countries. He had never been out of Stillwater. Not that he was unhappy. He had a nice little house of his own, a wife whom he loved dearly, and two children, named Janie and Bill. Still, it would have been nice, he often thought, if he could have seen something of the world before he met Mrs. Popper and settled down. He had never hunted tigers in India, or climbed the peaks of the Himalayas, or dived for pearls in the South Seas. Above all, he had never seen the Poles.

That was what he regretted most of all. He had never seen those great shining white expanses of ice and snow. How he wished that he had been a scientist, instead of a house painter in Stillwater, so that he might have joined some of the great Polar expeditions. Since he could not go, he was always thinking about them.

Whenever he heard that a Polar movie was in town, he was the first person at the ticket-window, and often he sat through three shows. Whenever the town library had a new book about the Arctic or the Antarctic—the North Pole or the South Pole—Mr. Popper was the first to borrow it. Indeed, he had read so much about Polar explorers that he could name all of them and tell you what each had done. He was quite an authority on the subject.

His evenings were the best time of all. Then he could sit down in his little house and read about those cold regions at the top and bottom of the earth. As he read he could take the little globe that Janie and Bill had given him the Christmas before, and search out the exact spot he was reading about.

So now, as he made his way through the streets, he was happy because the day was over, and because it was the end of September.

When he came to the gate of the neat little bunga-low at 432 Proudfoot Avenue, he turned in.

"Well, my love," he said, setting down his buckets and ladders and boards, and kissing Mrs. Popper, "the decorating season is over. I have painted all the kitchens in Stillwater; I have papered all the rooms in the new apartment building on Elm Street. There is no more work until spring, when people will want their houses painted."

Mrs. Popper sighed. "I sometimes wish you had the kind of work that lasted all year, instead of just from spring until fall," she said. "It will be very nice to have you at home for a vacation, of course, but it is a little hard to sweep with a man sitting around reading all day."

"I could decorate the house for you."

"No, indeed," said Mrs. Popper firmly. "Last year you painted the bathroom four different times, because you had nothing else to do, and I think that is enough of that. But what worries me is the money. I have saved a little, and I daresay we can get along as we have other winters. No more roast beef, no more ice cream, not even on Sundays."

"Shall we have beans every day?" asked Janie and Bill, coming in from play.

"I'm afraid so," said Mrs. Popper. "Anyway, go wash your hands, for supper. And Papa, put away this litter of paints, because you won't be needing them for quite a while."

THE VOICE IN THE AIR

THAT EVENING, when the little Poppers had been put to bed, Mr. and Mrs. Popper settled down for a long, quiet evening. The neat living room at 432 Proudfoot Avenue was much like all the other living rooms in Stillwater, except that the walls were hung with pictures from the *National Geographic Magazine*. Mrs. Popper picked up her mending, while Mr. Popper collected his pipe, his book, and his globe.

From time to time Mrs. Popper sighed a little as she thought about the long winter ahead. Would there really be enough beans to last, she wondered.

Mr. Popper was not worried, however. As he put on his spectacles, he was quite pleased at the prospect of a whole winter of reading travel books, with no work to interrupt him. He set his little globe beside him and began to read.

"What are you reading?" asked Mrs. Popper.

"I am reading a book called *Antarctic Adventures*. It is very interesting. It tells all about the different people who have gone to the South Pole and what they have found there."

"Don't you ever get tired of reading about the South Pole?"

"No, I don't. Of course I would much rather go there than read about it. But reading is the next best thing."

"I think it must be very boring down there," said Mrs. Popper. "It sounds very dull and cold, with all that ice and snow."

"Oh, no," answered Mr. Popper. "You wouldn't think it was dull if you had gone with me to see the movies of the Drake Expedition at the Bijou last year."

"Well, I didn't, and I don't think any of us will have any money for movies now," answered Mrs. Popper, a little sharply. She was not at all a disagreeable woman, but she sometimes got rather cross when she was worried about money.

"If you had gone, my love," went on Mr. Popper, "you would have seen how beautiful the Antarctic is. But I think the nicest part of all is the penguins. No wonder all the men on that expedition had such a good time playing with them. They are the funniest birds in the world. They don't fly like other birds. They walk erect like little men. When they get tired of walking they just lie down on their stomachs and slide. It would be very nice to have one for a pet."

"Pets!" said Mrs. Popper. "First it's Bill wanting a dog and then Janie begging for a kitten. Now you and penguins! But I won't have any pets around. They make too much dirt in the house, and I have enough work now, trying to keep this place tidy. To say nothing of what it costs to feed a pet. Anyway, we have the bowl of goldfish."

"Penguins are very intelligent," continued Mr.

Popper. "Listen to this, Mamma. It says here that when they want to catch some shrimps, they all crowd over to the edge of an ice bank. Only they don't just jump in, because a sea leopard might be waiting to eat the penguins. So they crowd and push until they manage to shove one penguin off, to see if it's safe. I mean if he doesn't get eaten up, the rest of them know it's safe for them all to jump in."

"Dear me!" said Mrs. Popper in a shocked tone. "They sound to me like pretty heathen birds."

"It's a queer thing," said Mr. Popper, "that all the polar bears live at the North Pole and all the penguins at the South Pole. I should think the penguins would like the North Pole, too, if they only knew how to get there."

At ten o'clock Mrs. Popper yawned and laid down her mending. "Well, you can go on reading about those heathen birds, but I am going to bed. Tomorrow is Thursday, September thirtieth, and I have to go to the first meeting of the Ladies' Aid and Missionary Society."

"September thirtieth!" said Mr. Popper in an excited tone. "You don't mean that tonight is Wednesday, September twenty-ninth?"

"Why, yes, I suppose it is. But what of it?"

Mr. Popper put down his book of *Antarctic Adventures* and moved hastily to the radio.

"What of it!" he repeated, pushing the switch. "Why, this is the night the Drake Antarctic Expedition is going to start broadcasting."

"That's nothing," said Mrs. Popper. "Just a lot of men at the bottom of the world saying 'Hello, Mamma. Hello, Papa.'"

"*Sh!*" commanded Mr. Popper, laying his ear close to the radio.

There was a buzz, and then suddenly, from the South Pole, a faint voice floated out into the Popper living room.

"This is Admiral Drake speaking. Hello, Mamma. Hello, Papa. Hello, Mr. Popper."

"Gracious goodness," exclaimed Mrs. Popper. "Did he say 'Papa' or 'Popper'?"

"Hello, Mr. Popper, up there in Stillwater. Thanks for your nice letter about the pictures of our last expedition. Watch for an answer. But not by letter, Mr. Popper. Watch for a surprise. Signing off. Signing off."

"*You* wrote to Admiral Drake?"

"Yes, I did," Mr. Popper admitted. "I wrote and told him how funny I thought the penguins were."

"Well, I never," said Mrs. Popper, very much impressed.

Mr. Popper picked up his little globe and found the Antarctic. "And to think he spoke to me all the way from there. And he even mentioned my name. Mamma, what do you suppose he means by a surprise?"

"I haven't any idea," answered Mrs. Popper, "but I'm going to bed. I don't want to be late for the Ladies' Aid and Missionary Society meeting tomorrow."

Priya Patel

Eliot Schrefer

is a *New York Times* bestselling author and has twice been a finalist for the National Book Award for Young People's Literature. His books have been named to the NPR Best of the Year list, the ALA Best Fiction for Young Adults list, and the Chicago Public Library Best of the Best. His work has also been selected to the Amelia Bloomer List, recognizing the best feminist books for young readers. He lives in New York City, where he reviews books for *USA Today*.